FLESH & BLOOD

by Angela Roquet

Blood Vice
Blood Vice
Blood and Thunder
Blood in the Water
Blood Dolls
Thicker Than Blood
Blood, Sweat, and Tears
Flesh and Blood
Out for Blood

Lana Harvey, Reapers Inc.
Graveyard Shift
Pocket Full of Posies
For the Birds
Psychopomp
Death Wish
Ghost Market
Hellfire and Brimstone
Limbo City Lights (short story collection)
The Illustrated Guide to Limbo City

Spero Heights
Blood Moon
Death at First Sight
The Midnight District

Haunted Properties: Magic and Mayhem Universe
How to Sell a Haunted House
Better Haunts and Graveyards

other titles
Crazy Ex-Ghoulfriend
Backwoods Armageddon

FLESH & BLOOD

BLOOD VICE BOOK SEVEN

ANGELA ROQUET

VIOLENT SIREN PRESS

For Paul and Xavier,

who make my world go round.

Chapter One

I could not get my fangs to suck back up into my gums.

I crinkled my nose and tried to think of unappetizing things, but all I could come up with was cold cow's blood. A line of drool spilled over my bottom lip, thanks to my mouth hanging open like an idiot. I wiped it away with the sleeve of my coat and made a slurping noise that only kids who wore retainers had a good excuse for.

The bedroom closet in Casey Poe's apartment was dark, but enough light seeped through the slats on the door that Mandy took notice of my condition. The whites of her eyes swelled as she glared at me.

"You didn't drink enough blood before we left," she accused in a razor-sharp whisper.

"Did, too."

"I told you to have a second pot."

"I had three," I hissed.

"Must be the adrenaline then," Mandy said, her voice dropping lower. She readjusted herself in the small nook we'd made between the hanging clothes. "You haven't been out of the house in a good while."

I nodded, refraining from speaking again as my elongated eyeteeth made the act uncomfortable. Besides, if I accidentally cut my lip and spilled fresh blood, our hiding spot would be blown all to hell. The werewolf we waited for would scent us long before he entered Casey's apartment.

I still wasn't convinced that the activated carbon we'd dusted our clothes with would fix that, but Mandy had insisted that it would make any lingering traces of us smell like ancient history. She'd also said that the pile of dirty laundry on Casey's bed was strong enough to draw flies from the next state over.

Thank goodness the girl was such a shitty housekeeper. At least breathing through my mouth meant that I didn't have to endure the odorific fog hanging in the air.

Mandy squinted down at her watch. Again. Her nerves were just as itchy as mine. We'd both be getting our asses chewed when we returned to the duke's manor—though if our suspect made an appearance tonight, the backlash would be tenfold.

Can't have your blood and drink it too, I reminded myself. Saving the day—or night—was worth the royal reaming that was sure to follow.

Casey Poe was Phillip Salinger's daughter. The half-sired minion Kassandra had sent to kill Dante's potential scions had knocked up another donor-in-training at the blood finishing school he'd attended as a teen. Casey's mother had died giving birth. She'd never outed him as the father, and he'd decided not to officially claim the child—not after being accepted into the personal blood harem of the Duchess of House Lilith.

As sleazy as that made Phillip in my book, I respected him for keeping tabs on the girl. Dante had granted me access to Blood Vice's resources and permission to investigate after Phillip and Kassandra had been coffin-locked. I wanted to know how the duchess had done it—how she'd convinced someone to commit such awful crimes and forfeit their life for hers.

Was it blind devotion? Blackmail? Hypnosis?

Between Blood Vice's private DNA library, their back door into Interpol's DNA database, and Phillip's online search history, I'd pieced together the big picture.

Casey's youth had been far from ideal. She'd played musical foster homes until her seventeenth birthday, then dropped off the grid until five years later when she ended up in a Chicago hospital after being viciously raped and left for dead. The news article about the incident mentioned a series of similar attacks in the area, and the only other survivor had been murdered the day after she was released from the hospital.

The creep was covering his tracks. Blood Vice only stepped in if a crime was glaringly supernatural or wild animals were suspected, especially in a big city. By not shifting, the creep managed to keep the evidence within human jurisdiction—until I'd taken a closer look at Casey's lab results.

Spawning non-consensual werewolves was punishable by death. If the guilty party wasn't pledged to a pack, then the sentence was carried out by the Vampiric High Council.

A second article that turned up in Phillip's search history detailed how Casey had made a miraculous recovery before going missing from the hospital. From there, she dropped off the grid again, though Phillip's bank accounts were noticeably lighter from then on as the statements proved.

He'd sent gift cards for groceries, signed her up for a subscription to a butcher box under a fake name, and made rent and utility payments for the apartment—which, while not the fanciest of abodes, was close to a conservation area where Casey could run during full moons. Phillip had taken care of everything for her.

Right up until All Hallows' Eve when he'd been laid down for a long, velvety nap.

I should've turned the information over to the duke and Blood Vice. But the last time Dante had allowed me to help with a case had been…*anticlimactic*. He'd pulled me at the first sign of progress—after *I* had made a significant discovery. Like snatching a baby bird out of the sky before it could fly more than two feet from the nest.

I couldn't stomach that again. Not after all the time I'd spent training to be part of Blood Vice. Not after all the legwork I'd put into this investigation. It was ridiculous. Frilly dresses and regal balls were nice, but I *belonged* out here, where I could make a difference.

Besides, it wasn't as though any of House Lilith's enemies knew what Mandy and I were up to tonight. No one did. We'd kept the simple yet brilliant plan we'd hatched to ourselves for days. Tonight, it was just us—well, us and the big, bad werewolf prying open Casey's bedroom window.

I still couldn't close my mouth, but I held my breath and silently begged my pulse to find somewhere other than my ears to do its relentless thundering.

Mandy stood perfectly still beside me, eyes level with a gap in the closet door slats. The skin between her brows creased, and I realized that she hadn't expected this to work. Hell, *I* hadn't expected it to work. What kind of creep-o stalker responded this quickly to bait? And years later, at that.

Red flooded my vision, and the man's outline came into view as he hooked a leg over the windowsill and climbed inside the apartment. The fire escape stairwell rattled behind him, and he paused, tilting his nose into the air.

Even from the closet, I could smell the tequila that saturated Casey's bed sheets. We'd found it in her kitchen and helped ourselves. It was a nice touch, considering the false DUI claim included in the carpool requests I'd posted online—after sending Casey off on an all-expenses-paid cruise to the Bahamas.

At least someone was enjoying my life's savings.

When tall, dark, and creepy closed the window behind him, my grip tightened around the silver-pronged stun gun I'd brought with me. My coat felt uncomfortably light, considering that I usually kept a .40 handgun in each breast pocket. But shooting up an apartment in north St. Louis would involve the human police. We would have hell to pay with the duke as it was, so I'd resigned myself to the stun gun.

Mandy's eyes took on a golden sheen as the man angled toward the closet. She could shift in a matter of seconds, but I had a feeling it wouldn't be fast enough to keep us out of Shit Creek if this guy decided that he wanted our hiding spot.

As his head turned back toward the bed, drool oozed from the corner of my mouth, and I instinctively slurped. It was just a small sound, but for a werewolf, it might as well have been a fire alarm.

I shoved Mandy into the shadowy corner of the closet— under the longer items of clothes and behind a cheap wicker hamper—just before the closet door was ripped open. It smacked the bedroom wall and rattled as if it might break right off its hinges.

Then a fist connected with my jaw.

My mouth snapped shut at the impact, and both fangs punctured the flesh of my bottom lip. Hot blood filled my mouth and dribbled onto my chin. The man's yellow eyes glowed in the dark as he sucked in a deep breath through his nose.

"Vampire," he whispered.

I expected the revelation to spook him, but something in his tone suggested that he was more intrigued than threatened. I covered my aching mouth with one hand and thrust the stun gun at his chest, but he caught my wrist, leaving the silver prongs crackling in mid-air.

"Are you here for my girl?" he asked, taking hold of my opposite wrist and prying my hand away from my mouth.

"She's not your girl." I spat the words at him, dotting his face with my blood as he pulled me out of the closet.

Though the room was dark, the Eye of Blood picked out the man's every detail—the thin mustache, a chipped front tooth, and a receding hairline. He drew my arms apart, forcing me closer to him so he could take another whiff.

"Mmm," he moaned. "You have a weakness for the she-wolves."

I took the opportunity to jam my knee into his groin. Fair fights were for the sparring ring.

A human would have released me and crumpled to the ground. Not this guy. A slow, rolling growl that sounded more like a purr rushed past his lips.

"I prefer humans myself," he said, tightening his grip on my wrists until I felt something pop. "I've never had a bloodsucker."

Then he wrenched me off my feet. The tips of my boots grazed the ceiling. Half a second later, my back flopped heavily onto Casey's cheap mattress, and all the air left my lungs.

Before I could regain my breath, the werewolf was on top of me. His thick legs straddled mine, effectively pinning me to the bed. Another grating purr echoed in my ears as he lowered his face to mine, lapping at the blood that had spilled from my mouth and trailed across my cheek. His weight pressed me deeper into the mattress, and I wheezed out a pathetic noise in protest.

The joints in my wrists felt loose. My hands and fingers tingled at the lack of circulation, but I hadn't dropped the stun gun. I squeezed the buttons on either side of the device, taking comfort in the motion despite its uselessness. The werewolf still had a hold of my wrists, and now my arms were stretched over the booze-soaked mounds of Casey's laundry.

Just as the creep's tongue reached the corner of my mouth, he paused and lifted his head, sniffing the air. I feared that he'd finally figured out that Mandy's scent wasn't coming from me but rather the closet where she was likely mid-shift. But then I smelled it, too.

Smoke coiled up from the dirty socks and tee shirts on the bed beside us. I stared at it, just as confused as my assailant—until I realized how close my hand with the stun gun was. The clothes suddenly ignited, and we both gasped as flames reached for our faces.

I tried to roll onto my side away from the fire, but I couldn't move. As alarmed as he was, the werewolf refused to let go of me. I wasn't going anywhere.

He brought my wrists up over my head and tried to secure them in one of his meaty hands. I didn't make it easy for him, which earned me a sharp slap once he managed the feat. Then he attempted to snuff out the fire with one of Casey's pillows.

I squeezed the stun gun again, angling the prongs down at the stretch of mattress above us. Without the pile of clothes for cover, the werewolf noticed this time.

"Sneaky bitch." He abandoned the small fire to reach for the device, but he didn't quite make it.

The bed jolted, and then Mandy in her dark wolf form was on the guy's back, teeth sinking into his shoulder. The man garbled out a broken scream then balled his free hand into a fist and punched Mandy in the muzzle. A whine punctuated her growl, but she held on, jerking her head as she tried to pull him off me.

I bucked my hips, hoping to unbalance the creep. The flaming pile of clothes burned brighter, spreading now that it had been left unattended. It made our shadows dance across the walls of Casey's room and painted a film of slick sweat over my skin.

I ignored the throbbing pain in my wrists and groaned through clenched teeth as I strained to pull my hands apart. The werewolf's grip was failing, thanks to Mandy and the fire.

One hand finally sprang free. The creep let go of my other to grasp at the stun gun, but Mandy gave his shoulder another yank. His hand came down on my face instead. My bottom lip seared with fresh pain as he clawed at me, and I felt the pads of his fingertips roughen against my skin.

He's attempting to shift. My mind exploded with panic. We were having a hard enough time with him in human form. As a wolf, he'd be ten times worse.

I stabbed the stun gun into the male's chest. The silver prongs ripped holes in his shirt, and his eyes faded from yellow to dark brown as I lit up his world. My fingers shook violently, but I had enough strength left to squeeze the device until the asshole started foaming at the mouth.

Mandy pawed my arm and yipped at the fire. She pressed her muzzle into the man's arm as he slumped and began to slide off me, pushing him toward the flames. She intended to use his limp body to put out the fire. At least one of us still had their head screwed on right.

I did what I could to help. The man's chest flopped onto the bed beside me, covering the bulk of the retail kindling and blowing hot ash in my face. I scrambled off the bed to the opposite side of the room before hacking up my lungs.

Mandy shifted and used Casey's pillow to put out the rest of the flames. When she was done, she clicked on the bedside lamp. Her naked body was spattered with blood and soot, yet she crinkled her nose at the mess I'd made of Casey's bed.

I wondered how Blood Vice would cover this up for our unaware host. She was a wolf, so maybe the truth wasn't entirely out of the question. All I knew was that my work here was done.

"So…" Mandy said, taking in the charred sheets and unconscious werewolf. "High-five now? Or later after we call this nightmare in and survive the aftermath?"

"Later. Much later," I said, rotating my bruised wrists.

I was already debating whether I should use my mild injuries to gain sympathy from the duke. I'd receive none from my sire. But whatever cross words they had for me was a small price to pay for what Mandy and I had accomplished tonight.

That's what I told myself anyway as I watched Mandy retrieve her cell phone from her abandoned coat and punch in Dante's number.

Chapter Two

Dante and I had our fair share of arguments. Of course, this was our first one as a married couple. He'd surprised me with a counterfeit marriage certificate, and a pretend proposal last week as an early Imbolc gift. My House Lilith name change was official, and I had access to my savings again.

Just in time for operation zap-a-wolf.

"I should have known you were up to no good when I saw this on the bathroom counter," Dante said, handing the diamond and sapphire band to me without making eye contact. He was in one of his nicer black suits. I had intentionally chosen tonight for the mission because of the extra meetings on his calendar.

The streetlights over I-270 flickered past the backseat window, outlining Dante's profile every few seconds and accentuating the frown lines that pulled at the corners of his mouth. I'd made peace with the fact that he would not be happy with me for sneaking out of the manor to play vigilante, but his disappointment still stung.

After the responding Blood Vice agents had fed me a blood bag and wrapped my wrists, Dante had ushered me into the back of the car and ordered the driver to take us home.

Mandy stayed behind to finish answering questions and to fill out our report. She also wanted to be on the wagon that was set to deliver our catch—Gordon Wikes, according to the wallet we'd found in his back pocket—to his last known pack alpha in Chicago. I would have given just about anything to be with her right now instead of here.

I sighed and put the ring on, wincing as the cold metal slid over my swollen knuckle. "I didn't want to lose it or get it dirty," I said. When Dante still refused to look at me, I added, "You can't seriously be mad at me for not wearing a *fake* wedding ring to take down a killer werewolf—"

"Fake?" His furious gaze latched on to mine. *Well, that did the trick.* "Fake! That ring is worth more than this car."

"Good God." I held my hand out to get a better look at the glitzy band. "Why would you spend that kind of money on a bogus bride?"

"I spent that kind of money on *you*," he countered. "It is a gift worthy of a duchess—even if you refuse to act like one."

"Hey, I didn't sign up for this gig," I reminded him. "I didn't spend three months in Denver training to sit on my ass and wear overpriced jewelry."

"What would you have me do, Jenna?" His voice took on a raw edge that made my stomach clench with guilt. "Shall I tell the queen and council that you have refused the sire appointed to you? What do you suppose will come of that?"

I gritted my teeth and turned to glare out my window. "I did a good thing tonight. You can't convince me otherwise."

"It was a good thing that someone less important could have done."

"Someone less important." I laughed. "Do you hear yourself?"

"Someone less important to *me*," he amended. "Someone less important to our *enemies*."

"Our enemies are all boxed up in coffins in the queen's basement."

Dante's hand wrapped around my thigh. He didn't have to call me out. We both knew it wasn't the truth.

"I am not your sire," he said softly, reminding me that the worst of my night was yet to come. "It is not for me to decide your punishment. And it is not within my rights to intervene."

Many of the vampires in House Lilith had been selected for some creative talent or another. The queen, Lili, was said to have been exceptional at beadwork and crafting headdresses among her tribe. Kassandra, the diabolical former duchess, had been a ballerina, and Alexander, the sire she shared with Dante, had been among the New World's first professional stage actors—before the uptight colonists began outlawing them and chased most of Alexander's company off to Jamaica.

Ursula had been chosen for her singing voice, though I was positive she'd missed her calling as a theater diva. The only thing she could pull off better than a poker face was a full-blown meltdown.

I found her waiting for me in the foyer, pacing back and forth in front of the double doors that led to Dante's office. Her red mane was tangled on one side, and she clutched a bloody espresso cup that she immediately threw upon seeing me. I ducked just in time, though blood and bits of ceramic peppered my coat as the cup shattered against the wall behind me.

"Insolent child," she hissed. "Ungrateful peasant."

I could always tell how pissed she was by the number of broken items in a room and the archaic nature of her insults. The cup she'd aimed at my head wasn't the only one littering the hardwood floor. The remnants of at least three others were scattered beneath Audrey's piano bench and under the towering Christmas tree in the opposite corner.

Dante sighed and handed me a handkerchief from his breast pocket. Then he retreated and took a seat at the piano, presumably to protect it from Ursula's tantrum.

"I won't apologize for my good deeds," I began, wiping at the dots of blood on my coat. It was pointless. The blood from earlier had already dried, and I wasn't even sure if a quality dry-cleaner could save the garment now.

"Where is that filthy mutt of yours?" Ursula demanded. "I'll have you begging for mercy before dawn."

"Leave Mandy out of th—"

Ursula's hand closed around my throat, cutting off the sentence before I could finish it. She was as fast as any werewolf, but I guessed that came with age. Her eyes filled with black, and she screamed in my face, revealing her extended, pearly fangs.

"I am your sire," she said. "You will do as I say."

I gurgled an incoherent reply and tried to swallow as my heels came up off the floor. My hands instinctively went to Ursula's wrists. She hadn't resorted to violence in some time, but then again, I hadn't given her any reason to.

My gaze darted to Dante.

"He cannot help you, vampling." Ursula squeezed my neck until her long nails bit into my flesh. "You are *mine*."

"S-s-sorry," I whimpered, straining to get the word out. I was too startled to be ashamed at how quickly I'd eaten my words.

"What was that? I cannot hear you, *Your Grace*." Ursula lifted me higher until only my toes touched the floor.

"*Sorry*," I said again, choking on the word.

"That's better." She dropped me. "Now. Your pet wolf?"

"I apologized," I rasped, still trying to catch my breath.

"Do not make me ask again."

"She is with Blood Vice," Dante answered. "Delivering the fiend they apprehended to Chicago."

"You sent her away on purpose!" Ursula accused.

Dante lifted his chin. We were in his house, but the princess still outranked him—for the most part. "She may be your scion's personal donor, but Agent Starsgard is also employed by Blood Vice, and therefore, mine to order about as I see fit."

"I would have done this with or without Mandy's help," I said, finding my voice again. When Ursula raised her hand to slap me, it took all my effort not to flinch. "Is this how Morgan gained your respect and obedience?"

Ursula's open hand curled into a fist, and she screamed. The gut-wrenching sound set my teeth on edge, and my eyes bulged. I took a careful step back, my boot crunching on the ruins of her tea service as she ripped out a handful of her own hair.

Maybe I'd gone too far, bringing up her late sire.

And then, just like that, it was over. An eerie, placid, nothingness smoothed Ursula's expression.

"I'm ordering a coffin. The next time you leave this house without my permission, you'll be sleeping in it instead of with your precious duke. Do you understand?"

I swallowed. "Yes, Your Highness."

Ursula left unhurried, as if in a trance, and headed for the north stairwell. I assumed that she was heading to Belinda's office to place her order. Either that or to the library to research what to do with a defective scion. I waited for her to round the landing and disappear before exhaling a trembling breath.

Dante clapped his hands to his thighs as he stood. "That went surprisingly well."

"Did it?" I rubbed my throat and glared at him.

"Shall I draw us a bath?" he asked, ignoring my irritation.

I supposed he thought turnabout was fair play. And how could I insist that he allow me to work with Blood Vice and then expect him to shelter me from the wrath of the princess?

"And perhaps order a pot of blood?" Dante added, taking in the mess on the foyer floor with a frown as he collected the handkerchief I'd dropped. I imagined that Belinda would be ordering new china along with the coffin. I shuddered, wondering how serious Ursula's threat had been.

Dante blinked at me, awaiting a reply. Some blood and a bath were exactly what I needed.

I nodded, unable to speak past the lump in my throat.

Chapter Three

I didn't know what to expect from Dante after Ursula's outburst. It would have been naïve to assume that he'd let the issue go, but he seemed content to set it aside, at least for the rest of the night. We enjoyed our blood and bath in silence and then settled into bed just before dawn.

By sunset that evening, my injuries were entirely healed. As a human, it would have taken weeks. I'd been a vampire for a year and a half, and I still couldn't get over how much my physiology had changed. I wasn't sure I ever would.

Much of the snow we'd received earlier in the month had melted, but a light dusting from the day coated the grass. Dante and I shared our first blood of the night on the patio behind the manor. It was freezing outside, but I enjoyed the fresh air. I had a feeling that Dante thought it would help ease my cabin fever.

Audrey tagged along, bundled in her new, baby blue coat and matching ear muffs. She'd received a teacup Pomeranian for Midwinter, and the thing had a bladder the size of a pea—which was fitting, considering she'd named the little hellbeast Sweet Pea.

Dante and I watched her chase the dog around the yard in the slight glow of the string lights decorating the roof. We were set to leave for Imbolc in a week, and Dante had promised his pending scion that the holiday decorations wouldn't come down until then.

"Are you going to tell me how you managed to slip past security, or shall I start firing people?" Dante asked as he poured us each a second cup of blood.

I gave him a dry grin and stopped fiddling with the wedding ring. "Taking a page out of Ursula's book?"

"Excuse me?"

"You're threatening others to force my cooperation. Pretty manipulative, wouldn't you say?"

He set the blood pot down on the patio table and shrugged. "It is so hard to find quality help. I cannot fathom how you slipped past everyone last night, including the technician watching the cameras. I will have to start there, I suppose."

"Don't fire anyone." I heaved an annoyed sigh. "Mandy rolled me out to the garage in her luggage."

Dante didn't look convinced. His eyes remained on mine as he took a careful sip from his cup of blood.

"She's strong, and I'm…compactable," I explained further, pulling my knees up to my chest and hugging them.

"I see." He hitched an eyebrow. "And I assume this means Lane did not help Agent Starsgard with her luggage when he dropped her off at the office. Otherwise, he would have noticed something amiss."

"He offered to help," I said, rushing to Lane's defense. "Mandy told him to save his chivalry for the harem and that her blood was off-limits."

Dante huffed. "You two are quite the pair."

"Thanks."

"That was not a compliment, my dear." He gave me a level stare. "Though I must admit that it was rather clever of you to send Phillip Salinger's daughter off on vacation before you infiltrated and destroyed her home."

I refrained from thanking him for the backhanded praise and cleared my throat before taking a sip of blood. If Casey knew what Mandy and I had used her apartment for, I was sure she wouldn't mind one bit. In fact, I hoped she might even forgive me for cutting off her allowance from Daddy Dearest.

"Whatever savings Salinger has should go to her," I said, hoping the thought had already occurred to Dante. He nodded slowly, but a bit of the light faded from his eyes.

"I will have Belinda forward Ms. Poe's case file to Alexander's accountant."

The duke had not spoken to his sire since All Hallows' Eve when we'd blindsided him by revealing Kassandra for the snake that she was. Everyone knew that Alexander's second scion had been his favorite. She also happened to be his lover. The latter didn't seem to bother Dante, but the former was a bit of a sore subject.

I often wondered why Alexander had chosen Dante. The duke's artist medium of choice was photography, the most modern of House Lilith's talents. It had existed during the Civil War when Dante was turned, but it was still in the early stages. From the fancy Union uniform that Dante pulled out for special occasions, I was reasonably certain that photography had not been his mortal occupation.

I liked to think that the duke had been chosen for his military prowess. That photography was a postmortem hobby he'd picked up to pass the abundance of time he now had. Kind of like my charcoal and pastel drawings. It made me feel less of an anomaly within House Lilith. And it gave me hope that I might eventually find my place like Dante had.

I finished my blood and held out my cup for the duke to refill.

"I'm going to call Dr. Delph later and see what the chances are of getting Casey an invite to Spero Heights," I said, changing the subject in hopes it would ease Dante's troubled expression.

"I think that is an excellent idea," he agreed. "Perhaps the good doctor will have some advice to offer you, as well."

I rolled my eyes. "I don't need my head shrunk, least of all by a psychic."

Dante chuckled and then glanced across the lawn to

where Audrey stood, her back turned to the little puffball of a dog as it crapped in the mulch under a naked redbud. The future baroness looked positively mortified. She edged around Sweet Pea, blocking our view to give the dog more privacy.

"Perhaps Dr. Delph should have a look inside *my* head," Dante grumbled under his breath. "I do not know what possessed me to make such an absurd purchase."

I shrugged. "Audrey seems pretty happy about it."

"True." He sighed and turned back to me. "Though I fear we will have to be extra cautious in the weeks following Imbolc. She will never forgive me—or herself—if she slips up and eats the little devil."

Ugh. My eyes widened at the thought.

When I first rose and found Mandy in my house, she'd offered to bring me one of the neighborhood cats. That was before she'd warmed to the idea of opening a vein for me. I'd opted for cow's blood from the butcher shop instead. After having fresh human donors, the idea of anything else made bile rise in the back of my throat.

Of course, the bad aftertaste wouldn't be responsible for even half of Audrey's trauma if she devoured her teddy bear of a pooch. We'd have to kidnap Dr. Delph and move him into the manor permanently.

"Is your blood okay, Your Grace?" Audrey asked as she

neared the patio and took in my concerned face.

"It's not Spot—*I mean*, it's hitting the spot," I stammered as Dante shot me a wide-eyed glare.

Audrey blinked innocently at us, though she squeezed Sweet Pea tighter. "Well, it's past our bedtime," she baby-talked to the dog before looking back at us. "Goodnight, Your Graces." She curtseyed and headed inside.

Once she'd closed the patio door behind her, Dante's nostrils flared.

"You are impossible, Mrs. Lilosa."

I toasted him with my cup of blood. "Why thank you, Mr. Lilosa."

A sheepish grin tugged at my mouth, though my heart did a little flip-flop. I enjoyed the new title far more than *Your Grace*. *My dear* wasn't so bad, but *Jenna* was only nice to hear in the bedroom. If he used it anywhere else, it was a sign of trouble.

"Would you like to check the new cameras with me?" Dante asked, rearranging our empty cups on the tea tray as one of the harem staff emerged to check on us.

"I thought you had a meeting tonight."

"It has been rescheduled," he said, a hint of reprimand slipping into his silky voice. "Ursula is brooding, so I have volunteered to keep a closer eye on you since my security cannot be trusted to do so."

I groaned. "You're babysitting me? How romantic."

"Fret not, my dear. I intend to have a much closer eye on *all* of you before this night is through." His gaze dropped lower, and despite the bitter cold, my skin flushed. "But, cameras first," he said, standing up from the table and offering me a hand.

Midwinter at the duke's manor had been…awkward. In the past, I'd only celebrated Christmas with the Bankses, my late Vice partner's family. It had been a chore to pull off the first year after being turned, but I'd managed it with Laura's help.

Now that I was legally dead and a member of House Lilith, I didn't know where to begin. For the first time in my life, I couldn't count all my friends on one hand. Between the guards and the harem donors and the new royal fam, holiday shopping had been an anxiety-riddled nightmare. And it wasn't as though I could just purchase chocolates or bottles of wine for everyone—not when vampires and special-diet donors were in the mix.

Thankfully, Belinda had come to my rescue. Though I was rather proud of the one gift I'd picked out on my own— a set of high-end, motion sensor game cameras for Dante.

The duke mostly stuck to sunrise and sunset shots, captured with the aid of timers and weatherproof gear. I found it more ironic than poetic, but he was good. I'd give him that. The canvas prints that decorated the walls of the manor were swapped out with new shots every so often, and the old ones were either donated to charity auctions or put into storage.

Dante had been thrilled by my clever gift. I envisioned deer, foxes, owls, rabbits, and all manner of wild animals gracing next season's installment. Not that I didn't enjoy Dante's vibrant suns and melting skies, but after spending so much time cooped up in the manor, I was looking forward to some new scenery.

Of course, I'd failed to take the security staff's wolf population into account.

The first camera turned up a dozen identical images of a gray wolf pacing through the snowy trees. The second camera was marginally more interesting, catching a different wolf as it spooked a turkey from its roost, which in turn, startled the wolf. The poor creature's fur stood up on end, and as soon as his panic had passed, he hiked a leg and peed on the nearest tree.

I draped my coat over Dante's office chair and crinkled my nose. "Did you inform the staff before installing these cameras?" I asked, wondering how many more guards I could inadvertently get into trouble this week.

"Of course not. What fun would that be?" Dante opened the files for the third and final camera without looking up.

"This seems…invasive."

"The cameras are on my personal property. The guards are on my payroll, and they are well aware of the cameras near the house. Oh, my." He leaned away from the computer monitor as the first image loaded.

"Is that? *Ewww.*"

A massive whitetail stood between two oak trees. The male had had a recent run-in with another impressive buck—as made apparent by the second set of antlers tangled with his own, still attached to the other deer's rotting head.

"Well… You do not see that every day." Dante cleared his throat and clicked through the rest of the uneventful images. "Shall we check again tomorrow?"

"I'm not sure I want to know what other horrors are lurking around out there," I grumbled and slumped onto the edge of his desk. "Where are all the fluffy bunnies and foxes?"

"Perhaps we should move the cameras out farther?"

I shrugged. "You might know how to shop for a duchess, but I clearly don't know what I'm doing when it comes to picking out a gift for a duke."

"Nonsense," Dante said, tucking a hand between my knees. "While I may not hang that one in the foyer, it is by far the most *interesting* photo I believe I have ever taken." When I didn't say anything, his hand slipped up farther between my thighs. "We could top that if you would allow me to bring a camera into the bedroom."

"That one wouldn't be foyer-safe either," I said, inhaling sharply as his hand traveled even higher.

The idea of christening his desk was appealing—certainly a better distraction and waste of time than we'd managed so far tonight. I twisted toward him, bracing one boot on the edge of his chair. Then a loud knock sent me scrambling to my feet.

Dante looked amused. No one entered his office without express permission, but my human instincts were still intact, and getting frisky in the boss's office still ranked pretty highly on my scandal-o-meter.

"Enter," Dante called out.

One of the double doors cracked open, and Belinda poked her head inside. I was convinced that the heat in my face told her everything she needed to know about what we'd been up to.

"Apologies, Your Graces," she said under her breath. "Agent Skye—Mrs. Lilosa—" Belinda, like most of the household, was having a difficult time deciding how to address me, especially knowing how I disliked the royal honorifics.

"Jenna. Just Jenna," I told her. "Really, it's what I prefer."

"Jenna," she said, then pressed her lips together as if waiting for Dante to reprimand her rudeness. When he didn't, she made her announcement. "Your sister is here to see you."

Chapter Four

There was something surreal about seeing Laura in person and not on the television or in the tabloids. I hardly knew what to say to her, but that had more to do with the fact that I couldn't get a word in edgewise with her blubbering hysterics.

She snatched a fifth tissue from the box on Dante's desk and finally took a breath to blow her nose. Her red-lacquered nails were past due for a touchup, and blond roots showed at her crown. A frumpy black sweat suit completed her look. It made the jeans and knit sweater I wore look fit for the runway.

"Hollywood kicked you out?" I repeated, minus the colorful curse words Laura had used to punctuate the revelation.

"Yes," she wailed. "*And* he accused me of cheating on him. *And* he said he was going to kill off Anastasia van de Velde with bad sushi. Can you imagine? I'm ruined!"

Dante's brows arched. "Should we warn the authorities of this murder plot?" he asked.

I gave him a pained smile and shook my head. "Anastasia is Laura's character on *Henry's Courtroom*—the soap opera she stars in."

"Oh." Dante's lips snapped shut, and he leaned back in his chair, looking equally relieved and perplexed. He didn't ask about my sister often, especially not since my meltdown over the wedding invitation she'd sent to Mandy a few weeks back. I supposed I couldn't hold that against her now.

"I'm really sorry, Laura," I said, rubbing my hand in circles on her back as she sobbed. Duncan, her pet Chihuahua, whined from the pink carrier tucked between her feet. Laura's matching pink luggage was stacked out in the foyer.

Dante knew my sister was aware that my death had been faked, but we hadn't exactly discussed family reunions or sleepovers. The humans who lived at the manor were trained and well-accustomed to life with supernaturals—*royal* supernaturals at that. They knew the pecking order.

In Laura's world, she was at the top of the social ladder. If she pulled her drama-llama act with any of the vamps or wolves in the house, we would have problems. I thought of Ursula and how eager she'd been to take out her anger at me on Mandy. Then I wondered how much more pleasure she'd take from tormenting my own blood and likeness. I shuddered.

"I love you, Laura," I said, trying to figure out a tactful way to dissuade her from staying. "But I'm surprised you didn't crash with one of your friends in L.A."

"Those hags aren't my friends." She sniffled and turned to drop her head on my shoulder, stretching over the arms of the guest chairs in front of Dante's desk. "This was definitely a *family* emergency. Speaking of, where's Mandy?"

"Chicago, working. She should be back by tomorrow afternoon," I said. "Maybe I—or one of Dante's guards," I said, recalling Ursula's order not to leave the manor, "could check you into a hotel in the meantime."

Laura pulled away from me. Her eyes brimmed with fresh tears, and her bottom lip quivered. "You mean I… I can't stay here with you?"

I squeezed her arms, silently begging her to hold it together long enough for me to explain.

"It's just that, there are a *lot* of vampires and werewolves living here—"

"I did fine living with you and Mandy. For a whole summer."

"That was different," I said.

"I bleached my hair and punched your time card while you were dead to the world." Her voice rose, and she yanked her arms out of my grasp. "I directed traffic and ate *donuts* for you!"

Dante stood from his desk, drawing Laura's wrathful expression away from me. "You are welcome to stay here as long as you need," he said, opening his hands. "We are all family now, are we not?"

Laura finally relaxed. I rested my hands on her arms again,

sighing with relief. I still didn't like the idea of her being under the same roof as Ursula, but I appreciated Dante for extending the invitation. Maybe one night would be okay. I *had* missed my sister.

Laura sniffled again, trying to compose herself, and then her gaze dropped to the ring on my finger. Just when I'd thought we were in the clear.

"*What* is *that?*" she demanded, snatching up my hand to get a closer look. "Are you engaged? How could you not tell me?"

"It's…part of the cover for my new identity," I said, refraining from calling the ring *fake* again after Dante's earlier reaction.

"When's the big day?" Laura asked. The lines creasing her brow suggested that she was far from happy for me. Not with her own nuptials in the breeze.

"There won't be one. We already have a forged marriage certificate. Its only purpose is to keep up appearances for the humans," I added when she shot a confused glare at Dante.

"I gave my ring back to David." A tear rolled down Laura's cheek, taking a fair amount of mascara with it. "Well, I threw it in his face, anyway. The dirty rat bastard."

"Would you like me to call for someone to help move your sister's things into one of the guest rooms?" Dante asked, likely anticipating the next wave of waterworks.

I shook my head. "I can handle her luggage, and she can stay in my room." Until Ursula and I could manage a conversation without her breaking something, I wouldn't let Laura wander the manor unattended.

Dante gave me a hopeful glance as Laura and I stood to exit his office.

"I'll come find you before sunrise," I promised, picking up Duncan's carrier. Dante nodded.

Out in the foyer, Murphy, Belinda, and Lane stood in a circle. Their harsh whispers cut off as Laura and I emerged, and they turned to ogle us. My sister with her fiery hair and SoCal tan. Me with my golden locks and alabaster complexion. Despite our differences in coloring, we were still clearly twins. Though it had been some time since we'd drawn public scrutiny for it.

I ignored our audience and handed Duncan off to Laura.

"Anything I can help with?" Murphy asked as I grabbed the handle of one of Laura's pink rolling suitcases. I picked up a smaller one and handed it to my sister, ignoring her indignant huff, before picking up the last piece of luggage.

"Nope. We've got it," I said, waving him off. "We are women, hear us roar, etcetera, etcetera."

I ushered Laura toward the south-wing hallway. Even in sweats, she'd strapped on a pair of stiletto heels, and half a dozen shiny bracelets jangled on each of her wrists. The combination made more noise than a Clydesdale in a parade. And it made my heart race as we neared Ursula's room. I prayed that she was still in the library where she spent most of her time.

"God, slow down," Laura whined.

"No, you hurry up," I hissed back at her. "And keep it down. Not everyone runs on night-owl hours around here."

I stole a glance at Audrey's closed bedroom door. A soft growl echoed from Duncan's carrier as if he could smell Sweet Pea. I shushed the dog and let go of the handle of the rolling suitcase long enough to push my bedroom door open. I waved Laura in ahead of me.

Since Mandy was gone and I'd spent the day in Dante's room, my bed was still made. Laura set Duncan's carrier on the gray bedspread while I stacked her pink luggage in the corner by my drawing desk.

"Mandy said your new place was nice, but wow." Laura stroked the fur throw over the foot of my bed. Her wide, blue eyes took in everything—the canvas print of a pink and violet sunrise above my headboard, the spill of curtains pushed to one side of the sliding patio doors, the flat screen on the far wall. Then her gaze paused on the fire hydrant lamp on the bedside table, a birthday gift we'd purchased for our mother years ago when she worked with the K9 unit. It was out of place among all the sophisticated luxury, but it made the room *home.*

I cleared my throat. "Are you…hungry? Thirsty? I could have something delivered from the harem if you want."

Laura snorted. "The *harem?*"

I blushed. "It's not *that* kind of harem. They're blood donors."

"I figured. It just sounds so…scandalous."

"It's really not. More like a 24/7 health club," I said, twisting my fingers anxiously. "Look, there are some more important things you should know if you're going to stay here."

Laura rolled her eyes and turned away from me to open Duncan's carrier. The Chihuahua poked his nose out and sniffed my sister's hand. His eyelids were heavy as if he were still shaking off the effects of whatever sedative Laura had given him for their flight.

"Mandy already told me that you're boinking the boss," Laura said. "He's cute, but I'm so not interested in men right now—living or otherwise."

"Are you kidding me? That is *not* why I'm worried about you staying here."

Leave it to my sister to jump right to the soap opera clichés. She threw her hands in the air and blew out a dramatic sigh.

"I can't believe you're still not over me screwing Vin on

prom night—"

"Are you even listening to me?" I said through clenched teeth, trying to keep my voice down. "I'm *not* worried about you trying to grudge-fuck Dante. Even if you bleached your hair, he would know you're not me in a second."

"But you still think I'd try, don't you?" She folded her arms, daring me to admit it. If she didn't look like such a train wreck, I might have.

"Of course not, Laura. That was high school. You've grown so much as a person since then."

Okay. That was a bit of a stretch, but it seemed to pacify her.

"Then why are your panties in such a twist?" she asked, dragging Duncan into her lap.

"Ursula, my adopted sire… You remember me telling you about her?" I chewed my bottom lip and watched Laura closely, searching for the appropriate amount of fear. It wasn't there.

"Sure," Laura said, twirling one hand in the air. "The runaway princess with explosive PMS."

I refrained from asking if that sounded like anyone she knew. "Exactly. And Ursula is experiencing one of those nasty bouts as we speak. If she finds out that you're here, she might consider torturing you just to punish me. And when I say torture, I mean it in the most literal and Medieval sense of the word. Are we on the same page now?"

Laura snorted. "Your Duke Charming wouldn't allow something like that, would he?"

"Ursula outranks him, and he's not my sire. She is."

Laura was quiet for a minute, considering the warning. "I really don't want to be alone right now," she said, the melancholy slipping back into her voice. "And I really *have* missed you."

"I've missed you, too." I sat on the bed beside her and scratched Duncan behind the ears. "If you could just stay in my room, maybe she won't notice for a night or two. The walls are well insulated, but she's right next door." I nodded toward the princess's room then tilted my head in the opposite direction. "Mandy is on the other side, but she stays in here most of the time. She's going to be so psyched that you're here," I said, taking up Laura's hand and squeezing it as she blinked away a tear. Her thumb slid over my ring again, and her face crumpled.

"I really thought he loved me," she whispered. "But I guess it was all a publicity stunt. Some last-ditch effort to save the show."

"His loss," I said, meaning it wholeheartedly. Laura could be a pain in the ass, but Hollywood was the whole ass. And everything in it. I'd hated his guts from the first day I met him.

"I know I'm not Mother Teresa or anything," Laura said,

pausing to rub her free hand under her nose. "But he was such a jerk. You have no idea—"

Duncan whined and hopped up and down in her lap. It was cute, and I suspected that he was trying to console her until he pranced in a nervous circle and jumped off the bed.

"Shoot." Laura gasped. "He hasn't gone tinkle since before take-off."

"I'll take him out," I offered, still worried about Ursula catching sight of my sister.

"Thanks. I haven't gone tinkle since before take-off either," Laura said, doing her own little awkward dance as she stood and pointed toward the bathroom door.

I nodded and unhooked Duncan's leash from his carrier, quickly latching it on to his collar before leading him out through the sliding doors and onto the terrace. The backyard was quiet, but I made sure to direct him to a patch of lawn that I knew wasn't viewable from the library or Ursula's window.

When we returned, Laura was still in the bathroom. The door was cracked open, and a horrible retching noise echoed from within. If Ursula were in her bedroom, she was sure to hear it.

I unhooked Duncan's leash and tossed it on the bed before slipping inside the bathroom with Laura and easing the door closed behind me.

As a teen, there had been plenty of times I'd wished my sister would be knocked off her pedestal. Taken down a peg or two. But seeing her this way…hunched over the toilet in sweatpants and stilettos, her heart breaking and makeup running…there was no joy to be had in it.

I knelt on the tile floor beside her and pulled her hair off the toilet seat and out of her face. "I'm here. I've got you."

"I'm so stupid, Jenna," she wailed, her words echoing in the ceramic bowl.

"We all are when we're in love."

"But you knew all along," she said. "You knew he was trouble, and you tried to warn me."

"I was on the outside, looking in." I thought of Roman and pressed my lips together. "I don't know everything. I don't always take good advice either."

We sat there for another few minutes until her sobs and dry heaving finally subsided. When it seemed like the worst had passed, I knotted her hair in a loose braid down her back.

"Do you want me to see if there's some broth or chicken noodle soup in the harem kitchen?" I asked.

"Soup isn't going to fix this." Laura groaned and finally pulled her face out of the toilet. "I'm pregnant."

Chapter Five

Pregnant.

My brain refused to wrap around Laura's confession. I had a hundred questions, but I saved them all and focused on getting my sister cleaned up and tucked into bed. Duncan snuggled in beside her after giving Mandy's pillow a good sniff. Once they nodded off, I made a beeline for Dante's room.

I found him in one of the armchairs in front of the fireplace that dissected the wall of windows facing the backyard.

"My sister is knocked up," I blurted out, skipping right over polite greetings.

"Come again?" Dante dropped the business magazine he'd been reading onto the side table and blinked at me.

"There is a bun in her oven," I said, drawing my finger in a wide circle around my own stomach. "Baby on board."

"Oh… Congratulations?"

A conflicted noise pushed up the back of my throat, and I pressed the palm of one hand to my forehead. "I…don't know."

"Perhaps this will change things between her and the former fiancé."

"Should it, though?" I made a face. "He's not exactly

father material. Not exactly husband material either."

"You know this man well, I take it."

"Well enough," I grumbled and flopped onto the chair opposite Dante's.

To be fair, I'd only met David Steckleman in person twice. But I'd seen him on television plenty of times, walking the red carpet and giving behind-the-scenes interviews for *Henry's Courtroom*. He was a self-absorbed shmuck, and his relationship with my sister had been on-again, off-again for over ten years.

The only reason I hadn't broken out in song and dance when Laura announced that the wedding was off was because I was in shock. We'd gone nearly ten years without more than a few bitter phone calls before she returned to Missouri to plan my *first* funeral.

I hadn't expected to see her again so soon—outside of our one-sided, small-screen soap opera-viewing sessions that I shared with Mandy, Audrey, and, occasionally, even Ursula. I didn't think Laura had expected to see me for some time either—not even at her wedding, which she'd scheduled for midday on a yacht.

Dante's hand rested on top of mine. "My offer was sincere. Your sister is welcome to stay here for as long as she likes. Through her pregnancy and beyond, if need be." He retracted his hand at my horrified expression.

"In a house full of vampires? While she's with child? That's an *awful* idea. The thought of subjecting her to Ursula alone makes me see red—literally."

"The princess is perhaps a bit…volatile at times, but she is not a monster."

"That's exactly what she is," I countered. "That's what we *all* are. This is no place for a human infant."

Dante bristled and looked away from me. "You were an officer of the law before you were turned, an occupation that would be unnecessary if humans did not possess the capacity for evil, as well."

"Oh, humans suck plenty." I laughed dryly. "Hollywood would be a shit dad, but I wouldn't ever have to worry about him taking a bite out of my niece or nephew."

Niece or nephew. I was going to be an aunt. Being a vampire didn't change that. It was still sinking in, but a tiny niggling of excitement and dread stirred in my stomach.

"Do you really believe Ursula—or anyone in this household, for that matter—would harm a hair on that child's head?" Dante asked, gripping the arms of his chair. I'd offended him, but I wasn't wrong.

"Don't get all preachy with me, not when you're worried about your own scion eating her dog after she's turned."

Dante huffed an indignant sigh and pointed a finger at me. "That is different. She will be newly risen. Every vampling has growing pains, as you are well aware. And Audrey will be closely monitored until she has adapted to her new diet."

"Regardless, my sister will be out of here in a week, tops," I said, shifting away from the *why* and on to the *when*. It seemed the best way to detour from the rocky road we were currently headed down.

"Will she tell the child's father or attempt to raise it on her own?" Dante asked next, seeming equally relieved to abandon the argument.

I shook my head. "No idea. She's in pretty rough shape right now. I'll ask tomorrow."

He nodded, approving of my decision. If only he were more agreeable about the bigger fish I wanted to fry—like Wikes. Thinking of the wolf I'd grappled with the night before, I took the opportunity to steer the subject away from my sister.

"Any updates from Mandy or Blood Vice?"

"Cable left a message with Belinda," Dante said. He stole a glance at his watch. "They arrived after sunrise, and the pack meeting should be taking place at this very moment. I suppose we will know more soon."

According to Mandy, Wikes' former alpha would more than likely sic the entire pack on him. There wouldn't be so much as a bone or tuft of fur left when they were done. It was barbaric, but in Wikes' case, it felt like perfect justice. In fact, considering the coffin-lock sentence the extra-naughty vamps got, it felt like Wikes was getting off easy.

Supernatural punishment was extreme compared to how humans did things. I didn't always agree with it, but then again, I didn't care for some of the mortal methods either. There were more than a few human rapists and murderers that had been set free with no more than a slap on the wrist that I would've loved to have seen thrown to the wolves.

The history books in Dante's library suggested that pack traitors used to be cut loose and hunted down like common prey. That trend lost favor as technology advanced, and the risk of human discovery became too great. One too many video clips of wolves attacking a presumed human and it would be open season on our shifty allies. Now, if werewolves wanted a big game hunt, they stuck to deer or elk.

"The Chicago pack has invited Cable's unit to stay overnight and witness their ruling," Dante continued. "They leave in the morning. Agent Starsgard will relay the in-person follow-up report at dusk if you would like to be present." His lips curled into a reprimanding grin. "It is *your* closed case, after all."

"Yes, it is." I held his stare, refusing to cower or show any sign of shame. "I would love to hear Mandy's follow-up report."

Dante smirked. "Perhaps Ursula will be in a better mood

by then, as well."

My composure trembled at the mention of my sire, and I again thought of Laura and her delicate condition—and of Ursula's earlier threat. It had shaken me. "If she harms Mandy or Laura, I will end her."

"Choose your words wisely, Jenna." Dante's brow creased, and the teasing humor left his expression. "In the wrong company, that would be grounds for coffin-locking. Ursula is royalty."

"She's a royal pain in my ass."

"I imagine she would say the same of you, with your resistance to the structure she has worked so hard to provide."

Structure? I wanted to laugh, but Dante's serious tone killed the sound before it could pass my lips. Structure was for molding children. I supposed, at least compared to Dante and Ursula's extensive experience as vampires, I was very much a child in their eyes. Which did not sit well with me. *At all.*

"And what should I make of you, Your Grace?" I snapped. "You claim to care for me. If I were coffin-locked, what would you do? Leave me to rot?"

Dante's jaw flexed, and he raked a hand through his loose curls. I was testing his patience tonight, far more than I had in the few months since we'd become intimate, but I wanted to know where we stood. These new vampiric relationship standards had me a little out of my depth. Not that I'd been anything remotely close to a love guru when I was human.

Dante abandoned his chair to kneel in front of mine. He reached for my hands, but I pulled them away, choosing to fold my arms instead. Whatever excuse he planned to deliver, I likely wouldn't accept it with the grace he expected of his *duchess*.

"Jenna..." His outstretched palms rotated and fell on top of my thighs. I could feel their warmth through my jeans, but the thrill the touch sent through my stomach curdled at his disheartened sigh. "I could never play Clyde to your Bonnie," he admitted. "How can you not understand that when you, yourself, have fought so hard for a place on the right side of the law?"

I scoffed. "That was before I realized how jacked-up the vampiric legal system is."

"Yet you still desire to work with Blood Vice, as made evident by your recent activities."

"I desire to protect the innocent from murderous bastards like Wikes."

Dante's hands slid off my legs, and my breath tightened in my lungs.

"If you *ended* Ursula, then yes, I would accept the council's decision should they decide you belong in a locked coffin," he said. "Just as I would accept Ursula's fate if she harmed someone you care for."

I kept forgetting that Dante and Ursula had been family for a century and a half. Whereas I'd only been a member of House Lilith for the past year. There was history here that I hadn't even scratched the surface of yet, despite my lessons with the princess. I guessed I should have been grateful that Dante viewed us as equals when it came to the council's wrath.

It wasn't as if I were sincerely plotting Ursula's demise. Sure, I was pissed at her—like that was anything new. But threats aside, she hadn't done anything to render herself irredeemable in my eyes. *Yet.*

Dante rested his hands on my legs again. "I am the Duke of House Lilith," he said as if I'd forgotten. "As such, I have a responsibility to not only the thousands of employees who work for corporations operated by House Lilith, but also to the agents of Blood Vice who keep our kind safe, and to the noble households that maintain the integrity of our society. I would never position myself on the opposite side of the law from those who have sworn an oath of loyalty to *our* family."

I sighed and leaned back in my chair. "Points for honesty, I guess. Though I think I would have preferred a white lie."

"And what purpose would that serve?" For an ancient vamp, he was utterly clueless sometimes.

I hitched an eyebrow. "Admitting you'd ghost a girl if she broke the law isn't exactly an effective way to get her to remove her clothes."

"That is not at all what I said, and you have broken plenty of laws, my dear." He paused, and his eyes lit with amused understanding. "I do not know what this *ghosting* entails, but I would be delighted to bend you over my knee for your crimes instead. Would that serve to loosen your laces?"

"My laces? Do we have a foot fetish, Mr. Lilosa?" I sucked at the insides of my cheeks to keep my face from splitting into a grin as his fingers slowly slid up my thighs.

"*Corset* laces, Mrs. Lilosa," he whispered.

"I'm not wearing a corset."

"It's an expression."

I rolled my eyes. "An archaic one. And I think I'll pass on the corporal punishment."

Dante's bottom lip jutted out, though the smolder remained in his dark eyes. "Shall I swear to move heaven and earth to secure your affection, then? To shield your body with mine should the sun ever find us? To seek out the rarest blood virgins for you to sup upon?"

"Go back to the heaven and earth bit. That was nice," I said, the words cutting off with a sharp inhale as his hands reached my waist. His thumbs traced my hip bones. Then he pulled me to the edge of my seat, drawing another surprised breath from my lips as he rose up on his knees between my legs and pressed his body into mine. I promptly forgot everything we'd been talking about.

If Dante wanted to keep me safe and sound at home, this was the way to do it. If only life outside this room could just take care of itself. It probably could. But there was nothing lazy about the duke's actions—on either side of his closed doors.

My mouth opened in anticipation as Dante leaned forward, but instead of a kiss, he nipped my bottom lip and pulled away. He darted in again, briefly brushing his mouth against mine. Such a tease, my duke.

When he finally relented, I melted against him, humming my appreciation. His breath was hot against my face, sweetly tinged with fresh blood and minty toothpaste. His hands, too, radiated feverish heat through my ribcage as he explored under my sweater.

I lapped my tongue under his fangs, checking their evenness with the rest of his teeth. The discovery had perplexed me the first time I'd noticed it. We were both undead, so there were no pheromones to trigger the other to feed. It was both reassuring and…regrettable.

The irrational craving I'd experienced with Roman had been dangerous and euphoric. Dante was by far the superior lover, and I was absolutely over Roman, but I was beginning to understand why the queen preferred her human consorts. There was something irresistibly seductive about forging a blood bond.

Jumping out of perfectly good airplanes is equally as exciting and stupid, I reminded myself.

Dante slipped his hands under my thighs and lifted me out of the chair. I wrapped my legs around his waist as he circled the armchairs and carried me toward the bed, his mouth still devouring mine.

Blood bond or not, my body ached for Dante's touch. This flavor of love was safer, and it was still potent enough to sweep me off my feet and make me forget how to form words beyond moaning his name.

Chapter Six

Dante took my hand and pressed it to his chest, holding it there as his breathing steadied. I could feel the thrum of his heart as it slowed to a normal pace once again—well, normal for a vampire.

"Does it sadden you that you shall never have children of your own?" he asked.

It was a strange question, and my first instinct was to scoff at the idea of bringing up a child in the feral world we pretended to know our way around. But that hadn't gone over so well when I freaked about Laura doing that very thing, so I bit my tongue until my mind settled on a different response.

"I was twenty-eight and had just been promoted to Vice when I died. I hadn't really given kids much thought by then, and I haven't since." I shrugged. "Does it bother you?"

Dante tilted his chin down to meet my gaze and smiled softly. I never quite knew what to make of the way he looked at me. Did he appreciate my interest in his thoughts and feelings? Or did he think his replies were so predictable that I was a fool for not guessing them?

"I had a child before I was turned," he confessed, surprising me. "A wife, as well. Both were taken by pneumonia before the Civil War ended."

"I'm so sorry."

"It was a long time ago, and I hardly had the chance to know either. The marriage was arranged by our parents, and I was called away to Virginia before my son was born."

"Still…that's awful." I nestled closer to him, suddenly cold. No wonder he didn't talk about the past. I had so many more questions, but after such a tragic confession, I couldn't bring myself to ask them.

"Audrey will be a fine scion," Dante said, a more cheerful note entering his voice. He pressed a kiss to my forehead. "She is the closest I shall ever come to fathering a child again, and I am more at peace with that than I expected to be. But you"—he looked down at me—"you will have a new blood relative by birth soon. It is quite exciting and rare for a vampire to have a relationship with their living kin."

"Will the council have a problem with that?" I asked. "It seems a little much to expect a young child not to tell anyone about me."

"Children say all manner of curious things and are known to have imaginary friends," Dante said. "And I do not see why we would need to inform the council, so long as your family outings stay out of the public eye."

I nodded and laid my cheek against his chest, nestling my head under his chin. Maybe he was right. This could work. I could be a *real* aunt and watch the kid grow up in person rather than through stolen snapshots found in trash mags.

"And just think," Dante said, stroking his fingers down the length of my arm, "if your sister relocates to St. Louis and becomes a single mother, you will be too busy helping her rear the child to get into trouble—ooh!" He gasped as I pinched his nipple.

"Maybe you should worry more about keeping *yourself* out of trouble, Your Grace."

"Have mercy." Dante chuckled as he took my hand and pressed it flat to his chest again. He was teasing, but it wasn't a terrible thought, Laura staying in Missouri. Me helping her with the baby—during the night anyway. But a thought was all it would ever be.

"Laura is at the peak of her career," I said. "Once her character is killed off on *Henry's Courtroom*, she'll get all kinds of exclusive casting calls. A lot of the daytime soaps are even willing to work around pregnancies. But they can't work around her living halfway across the country."

"Pity." Dante gave me a comforting squeeze. Then he craned his neck back to get a look at the digital clock on the bedside table. "Two hours to sunrise, my dear. I suppose we should part ways to tend to our remaining business before settling in for the day."

I tucked my face into his shoulder and groaned.

"Come now." He combed his fingers through my hair and planted a kiss on my temple. "Your mortal sister will need to eat eventually. Belinda tells me the new catering service she hired specializes in nutritionally-dense dishes. I have calls I must return this night, as well, including one to an ally on the council."

"Fine." I sighed and slid off the bed, dragging the flat sheet with me. Dante laughed as I stole a glance back at his nude body splayed across the mattress. He caught a corner of the sheet and tugged me back to him for a kiss.

"You are shameless, Mrs. Lilosa."

"And you're delicious, Mr. Lilosa," I replied, stealing another kiss before handing him the sheet and searching for my clothes.

In the few hours before sunrise, while Dante finished returning his phone calls, I checked in on Laura and Duncan. I tracked down Murphy to remind him to update the day shift security staff and then made arrangements with the harem for breakfast and lunch to be delivered to my *private guest*. It wouldn't be too out of the way, considering Audrey often took her meals in her room, too. With Sweet Pea and Levi, her werewolf donor-in-waiting.

I liked Levi. Probably more than he deserved, but I'd handpicked him from Renfield Academy myself after

Audrey's first batch of dowry donors had turned out to be duds. It had been an early attempt of Dante's to make me feel like a respected member of our household, and I'd taken full advantage of the situation, picking out a young, charming candidate to turn Audrey's doe eyes away from the duke.

Levi was a good kid. He'd already proven himself as a worthy addition. Now, the trick was to make sure he didn't get so cozy with the future baroness that he turned her furry before Dante could sire her at Imbolc. One week to go. So far, so good.

Back in my room, I left my sister a note with precise instructions to stay put. I wasn't too worried about her safety during the day while the majority of the house was dead to the world, but I didn't want the whole harem knowing she was here. That seemed like the quickest way to alert Ursula.

While I *would* kill the princess if she harmed Laura, that didn't necessarily mean I *wanted* to. Certainly not if it meant a dark coffin that no one would save me from.

Part of me wanted to stand guard over my sister until dawn pulled me under, but waking up beside my corpse probably wouldn't be good for her delicate condition. Besides, I lived for dying in Dante's arms. The only thing better than that was rising with him at sunset.

I'd refused to let Vin sleep in bed with me during the day—of course, that had more to do with my fear that he'd conduct medical experiments on me while I was out. With Roman, I'd been under the thrall of our blood bond. That was the only explanation I had for the only time I'd let the sun come up with a mortal's arms around me.

I imagined he was used to it with Vanessa. I tried to push the ugly thoughts of the two of them out of my mind. None of that mattered now.

Sunrise with Dante was like slipping soundly into the very best dream. I took comfort in knowing that when my eyes closed and the dawn pulled me under, he was taking his last breath of the night at the exact same time. And sunset meant waking from that dream just as tangled in each other's embrace as when our spirits had departed to chase stars through the night until darkness led us home again.

Maybe we'd have this ritual for decades to come. I still hated to miss it even once. It was miserable enough whenever Dante traveled for business. Laura would have to understand, and once Mandy returned, she'd get over it.

Still, I stayed in my room for as long as I could, watching Laura snooze, sketching her restful form in one of my drawing pads. I pondered how long it would be before mortality caught up with her and we could no longer get away with twin-ish shenanigans.

Duncan woke once, and I took him outside again before changing into a pair of silk, bat-print pajamas Mandy had gifted me for Midwinter. I skipped the fuzzy bat slippers. Those I saved for our soap opera dates.

Half an hour before sunrise, I heard Ursula's bedroom door open and close. A moment later, it opened and closed again. Morning blood was being delivered. If I wanted mine hot, it was time to slip out. I did so quietly, locking the bedroom door behind me.

Dante was already changed into flannel pajama bottoms when I returned to his room. A steaming blood pot rested on the bedside table. He waved a hand at it, inviting me to help myself as he finished a phone call.

"I will pass on your kind words, Lord Carter. We are looking forward to spending Imbolc with your house, as well."

Lord Everett Carter oversaw the vampiric banking system. He was also a member of the Vampiric High Council, the supreme court of supernatural society, and had voted in Ursula's favor during her trial.

Dante gave me an impish grin and accepted the espresso cup of blood I handed to him. I sat on the edge of the bed before pouring one for myself.

"Rest in peace," Dante finally said before ending the call.

"Did you break the bank on this thing?" I asked, holding out my hand with the glitzy ring. "Is Lord Carter bumming over the missing funds in your account?"

Dante drank his blood in one go and refilled his cup before answering. "He was calling to enquire if we would be attending the queen's Imbolc celebration since we were missed at Midwinter and departed so early from the All Hallows' Eve ball."

"And to whom might you be passing on his kind words?" I asked, holding out my cup for a second helping of blood.

"You, my lovely bride," Dante said with a chuckle. "He wanted to offer his congratulations on your official name change and integration into House Lilith, and then asked after the large sum you spent on a vacation package to the Bahamas for one."

I nearly choked on my blood. "So much for privacy."

"Here, here." Dante toasted me with his cup. "Fortunately, I was able to explain the purchase on your behalf. Lord Carter was quite impressed."

I grinned and finished off my blood before handing Dante my empty cup. He set it next to his on the tray beside the bed. When we rose at sunset, it would be gone, taken away by one of the harem donors.

The duke was too trusting for my taste, but he was a generous and kind employer. I didn't fear any ill will from the harem—not even after what had happened with Yoshiko. Though Belinda was still looking for a suitable harem manager to take her place.

No one was quite as good as Yosh when it came to matching up vamps and donors, and her juice and smoothie concoctions were unbeatable, too—at least according to Mandy. Everyone seemed to be enjoying the new variety of food offered by Hearty Harem, though. The catering service had come highly recommended, and even got the stamp of approval from the wolf guards of the house—high praise to be sure.

Dante tucked himself into bed beside me and wrapped his arms around my shoulders. The sky beyond the glass wall and fireplace lit softly with the first colors of dawn. It was UV glass, but before the sky grew any lighter, the automatic steel shutters began to slide into place.

When I first moved into the manor, the shutters had only activated if the glass was compromised. But as the enemies of House Lilith became bolder, so too did our defenses. Now, the shutters sealed all vampire suites during the day.

My room would still be open for Laura to take Duncan outside since I'd put in the request with Murphy. But there would be a wolf or half-sired guard stationed outside on the terrace and in the south wing. I tried to let that soothe my anxiety as the rising sun sapped my consciousness.

"Everything will be fine," Dante whispered, sensing my uneasiness.

The shutters finished closing, and the bedside lamp

clicked off as it did every morning, five minutes before sunrise.

I wrapped my arms around Dante and sighed, hoping he was right.

Chapter Seven

Since joining Blood Vice, Mandy had curbed her girly ways. She didn't wear half as much makeup, and her civilian wardrobe was less colorful, too. She wanted to be taken seriously as an agent. and her young age made that difficult enough.

So, when she reported to Dante's office to give us her follow-up report with her hair in ringlets, wearing blue fingernail polish and electric green eyeliner, I knew she'd been home long enough for a lengthy reunion with Laura.

"Cable filed the official report with Captain Nicks this morning," Mandy said, frowning at my scrutiny of her hands before tucking them behind her back. "The Chicago alpha announced Wikes' known crimes to the pack. When he offered Wikes the chance to explain himself, the creep claimed that wasn't even half of his legacy."

Dante nodded. "It is a common tactic to buy time, hinting that he alone possesses knowledge we might be inclined to negotiate for, but that is not how Blood Vice nor pack politics works."

"Right," Mandy agreed. "Cable assured the pack—and Wikes—that we would continue the investigation post-mortem. He said the Cadaver Dogs' noses were more trustworthy than the word of a traitorous fleabag." Mandy snorted. "You should have seen the look on Wikes' face. He really thought he was going to delay the alpha's sentence."

"So, it's over, then?" I asked. "He's dead?"

Mandy nodded, and I sat on the edge of Dante's desk, relieved. One more evil prick was off the streets. Permanently. I didn't have to see his gory end with my own eyes to appreciate a job well done. Mandy looked satisfied by the outcome, and that was good enough for me.

Dante cleared his throat, ending our victorious moment of silence. "As much as I would love to praise your *heroic* actions, Agent Starsgard, I must insist that you not attempt anything like what you did Wednesday again."

"Oh?" Mandy shot me an I-told-you-so glare.

"I am well aware that this was not your idea," Dante went on. "But as your employer and the master of the house you are beholden to, I expect a certain level of loyalty from you. I would very much hate to be forced to fire or evict you."

"Really?" I stood and faced Dante, putting myself between Mandy and the desk. "Are threats necessary?"

"It's fine, Jenna." Mandy grabbed my arm and tugged me aside so she could see Dante. "At least he's being nicer about it than the princess. She offered to drain me dry if I ever put the duchess in harm's way again." From the tight line of her jaw, I knew that Mandy would shift and chew Ursula a new asshole before she let the princess's fangs near her flesh.

"I am *not* apologizing for what we did," I said to Dante before remembering how I'd done just that when Ursula flipped out. "Well, not to *you* anyway. Unless you plan on vamp-handling me like the princess did."

"Never." Dante blanched. "You must understand, Ursula has been through a great deal. She is fragile and still recovering from much loss."

"Fragile?" Mandy made a face. "I think the word you're looking for is unstable." Dante's sympathetic gaze narrowed, and Mandy fell quiet again.

I put my hands on my hips. "If you'd give me something more worthwhile to do, I wouldn't have to sneak around to solve the world's problems behind your back."

"If only it were so simple," Dante said. He sighed and drummed his fingers on his desk. "Be patient with Ursula. Given time, I am certain we can convince her to allow some...concessions."

"Time?" I rolled my eyes. "Sure, that'll fix everything."

"You are immortal, my dear. Time is the one thing you have in abundance."

"Having all the time in the world doesn't make wasting it any less infuriating."

"Then don't." The duke gave me a tight smile. "After all, your sister is visiting."

I huffed at the veiled dismissal and stormed out of

Dante's office without a goodbye. Mandy mumbled a quick, "Your Grace," before chasing after me down the south wing hallway.

I didn't like being mad at Dante, but when he put on the *lord and liege* hat, sometimes it was unavoidable. Sure, being diplomatic was great. Not smashing up the china and screaming like a banshee, that was swell, too. But treating someone I considered family as though they were nothing more than a disposable employee? Not cool.

"We knew this would happen," Mandy said, skipping to keep pace with me. "It's not exactly a surprise."

"It's still annoying," I grumbled. "Still pisses me off and makes me want to break something."

"Ursula's broken enough." Mandy's eyes widened as I stopped to give her a concerned once-over. "Not anything *new*—that I know of. I just heard about the mad tea party from the harem."

"Oh." I relaxed and resumed my path down the hall. "Where did you have your run-in with Her Royal High Maintenance?"

"The gym," Mandy said, then her voice dropped to a whisper. "I had the donor who delivered her first blood of the night let it *slip* that I was home and working up a sweat to make sure she steered clear of your room and Laura."

"Good idea."

"Did she tell you that she's—?"

"Yup."

"Then why the hell are you letting her stay here?" Mandy hissed.

I stopped outside my bedroom door and turned to glare at her. "You think I didn't try to change her mind?"

"Ursula belongs in a straitjacket."

"You're singing to the choir, Teen Wolf."

Mandy's nose curled at the nickname, but she ignored it otherwise. "I love your sister, but this is not a great time for a visit."

"Nope."

What else could I say? Laura never took anyone's advice, least of all mine.

Mandy blew out a frustrated sigh. "If the duke fires me, I'm going to make a trip out to California to eat Steckleman's face off. For real," she added with a pointed look.

"No one is getting fired, and eating your feelings isn't going to solve anything."

Mandy shrugged. "It might. You don't know."

I thought of Wikes and how the pack had gobbled him up. Maybe Mandy was right. But as much as I hated Hollywood for the way he'd treated my sister, he wasn't a rapist or a murderer. We couldn't just go around killing everyone we didn't like. I wasn't *that* bloodthirsty, even if I did view my new kind as monsters.

"Okay," I said, grabbing the doorknob. "Time for happy faces."

Mandy gave me a mocking smile and poked her finger into one of her dimples as we entered my room. At least we were on the same page about keeping the supernatural drama under wraps for Laura. She had enough on her plate right now.

Duncan greeted Mandy and me by racing around our feet and yipping his little head off. I shushed him and quickly closed the door behind us.

The overhead lights were out, but the ceiling fan was on. Odd for the dead of winter, but understandable with Laura's fiery temper and her morning sickness. I was more annoyed by the fact that she'd pulled the curtains over the patio doors closed, shutting out the darkness that brought me to life each night.

Our mother's lamp glowed softly on my night table. The rest of the room was awash in blue, thanks to the television that blared over the gagging and retching noises coming from the bathroom. I wasn't sure if the evening news or Laura's pregnancy was more to blame.

"An inside source claims there will be a shocking, major death before the final season of *Henry's Courtroom* concludes," a bubbly gossip anchor announced as a montage of Judge

Henry's many conquests played on a screen behind her. "Stay tuned for celebrity fan theories before tonight's episode."

"All things considered, should we be watching this right now?" Mandy asked as she seated herself on the edge of my bed.

"Don't change the channel," Laura called from the bathroom between dry heaves. "I have to know if they edited anything from the original script." She paused to pant a few shallow breaths. "There could be a clue as to how he plans to murder me."

"I thought he already told you it was bad sushi," Mandy said.

"That was just *his* dumb idea." Laura panted a few more times. "The show writers will probably come up with something better—or worse."

"Does it matter?" I asked. "Hollywood's a prick. Shouldn't you be posting fancy pictures of yourself living your best life on social media or something?"

"Check." Mandy wiggled her blue digits for me to admire. "I had the harem deliver O.J. in champagne flutes so we could pretend we were sipping mimosas, too. Just in case that creep has any concern at all for his unborn child."

"Oh, that's classy." I scooped Duncan up off the floor before he gave himself a heart attack from all his anxious prancing.

"You're my sister," Laura shouted from the bathroom. "You're not supposed to judge me."

The toilet flushed, and a second later, she appeared in the doorway in my bathrobe. Her mascara was a little puddly, but at least she looked better than she had the night before. Her hair was pulled back in a high ponytail, curled in ringlets like Mandy's. They'd had a girly makeover day while I was out. Not that I cared. Much.

"I really don't think it's healthy, given your condition"—I waved a hand at her midsection—"for you to be torturing yourself. We can record tonight's episode and watch it another time when you're less...emotional."

"Emotional?" Laura snarled. "You think *this* is emotional?"

"Here we go." I sighed and dropped Duncan onto the bed beside Mandy.

"Emotional would be slashing his tires." Laura's voice rose, taking on the dangerous lilt of Anastasia van de Velde whenever she broke into a monolog. "Emotional would be emailing the entire cast and crew the quote-unquote professional nudes he *gifted* me on my birthday." She made a disgusted sound in the back of her throat. "Because knowing her fiancé stripped for another woman is exactly what every girl wants on her special day. How could I not appreciate the artistic effort and thoughtfulness? Emotional would be spilling my guts to the tabloids about the love child he doesn't want anything to do with. How do you suppose the finale ratings would look if I did that?"

"Laura..." I folded my arms. "Anastasia van de Velde might be the kind of person who would use a child to spite a lover, but you're not." When she didn't answer right away, I swallowed. "Please tell me you're not that kind of person."

"Of course I'm not!" She clenched her fists and waved them in the air. "I'm just...blowing off steam. Okay? Could you maybe, I don't know, take a break from playing good cop for one minute and fantasize about revenge with me? *That* might make me feel better."

"Lord, have mercy," Audrey cried. The duke's pending scion stood in my bedroom doorway, draped in a velvet gown. "Is that *the* Laura Skye?" She gasped and squeezed Sweet Pea until the little dog squeaked in protest.

I'd been so wrapped up in my sister's outburst that I hadn't heard the door open. I shot Mandy an accusing look. Her mouth hung agape as if she'd been waiting for an opening, and one finger pointed toward the door where Audrey stood.

"Who's this? Ursula?" Laura demanded, tilting her chin in the air even as her pupils dilated. She'd never met the princess, and the only detail that Mandy or I had given her to go on was red hair. Audrey's strawberry locks were close enough to cause concern.

"I guess someone should have told Princess Pea that we were canceling the soap session," Mandy said. Then she snatched up Duncan as he caught sight of the puffball tucked in Audrey's arms. The hair along his back rose, and he growled, baring his teeth at the other dog.

"Canceling? Why?" Audrey asked, taking a timid step inside the room. Sweet Pea squirmed and whimpered in her grasp, but she held tight, covering the little beast's face with one hand. "What could be better than watching *Henry's Courtroom* with a star from the show? I'm Audrey, by the way," she said to Laura with a curtsey. "The soon-to-be Baroness of House Lilith."

My sister sniffed and whipped her ponytail over her shoulder before turning her cocky grin in my direction. "I can see why you were worried about this one with Duke Charming. Still wary of the redheads, huh?"

"Hardly." My face was on fire, but Audrey's hair color had nothing to do with my initial animosity toward her. Though, now that Laura had pointed it out, it was rather curious how redheads seemed to cause me the most grief.

"Duke Charming." Audrey giggled. "That's cute. I like it."

"Don't even *think* about calling him that," I snapped. "Or you'll be earning yourself a far less savory pet name."

The humor drained from Audrey's expression, and she

gave me a quick nod before dropping her gaze. It made me feel like a schoolyard bully, especially when Mandy's eyebrows shot up on her forehead. She was usually the bitey one with Audrey.

The silence grew uncomfortable, but then Duncan let loose with another series of yips.

"Shhh, Duncan Punkin." Mandy wrapped a hand around his muzzle to quiet him.

"I think you'll have to leave Sweet Pea in your room tonight," I said to Audrey, caving to the soap viewing before Laura turned it into a battle of wills. Audrey perked up instantly.

"Levi can watch our little fluff muffin tonight," she said, turning for the door. "I'll be back shortly, with popcorn—"

"No!" Laura gasped, then pressed a hand to her mouth. "No popcorn."

"Oh." Audrey gave her a confused look but nodded, eager to please the soap queen. "Okay."

Laura waited until Audrey closed the door behind her before racing back into the bathroom.

"This is not a good idea," I said under my breath to Mandy.

"Nope."

Less than five minutes later, the four of us were crammed together on my mattress, heads over the foot of the bed, chins in our palms as the opening credits for *Henry's Courtroom* began. Duncan did a lap around the room and yapped at the image of Laura on the television before wedging himself in between my sister and Mandy.

"Will the princess be joining us?" Audrey asked.

"Not tonight." I gave her a tight smile. "Maybe not next week either. Ursula is pretty ticked at me right now."

"Because you snuck out with Agent Starsgard?" Audrey laughed nervously at my glare. "The foyer…it echoes. Belinda let me pick out the new tea sets," she said, quickly changing the subject. But Laura wasn't having it.

"Snuck out?" she asked, turning to me. "Is this your home, or are you a prisoner?"

I shook my head. "It's not like that—"

"Are you sure that's not the Stockholm syndrome talking?"

"I'm supposed to be dead, Laura. I can't just skip through the mall whenever I want—certainly not in St. Louis."

"And House Lilith has many enemies," Audrey added, earning another glare.

"Not helping." I gritted my teeth and turned back to Laura. "We went to New York to watch the ball drop for New Year's Eve. We get out. Maybe not much, but we're not prisoners." I felt like I was trying to convince myself as much as my sister at this point.

Ursula hadn't said that I could *never* leave the house. Not even when she'd lost her cool in the foyer. She'd only told me not to go anywhere without her permission.

If I wanted a mall outing, there was a decent chance she'd say yes—in a month or so, after getting over this latest hiccup. And if I took half a dozen guards with me.

"Do you know who they intend to kill off?" Audrey asked, drawing my attention back to the television. "No, wait! Don't tell me. Oh, I sure hope it's not you."

It was nearly impossible not to dig for the inside scoop while all snuggled up with one of the show's actors. It seemed equally difficult for Laura to keep the secrets her contract stated she wasn't allowed to disclose, especially when she could use those secrets as currency to purchase some fangirl doting.

"I'm in three weeks' worth of taped episodes after this one," she confessed. "David's too cheap to scrap any shoots he doesn't have to, so Anastasia is safe until then."

"Spoiler alert." Mandy snorted and threw a pillow at Laura. When Laura went to throw it back, Mandy held up her hand and sniffed the air, nostrils flaring dramatically.

"Ursula?" I whispered, wondering how quickly I could stuff my sister into the bathroom.

"No. Just Dookie Dukerson," Mandy said, earning a pillow in the face from me right before Dante opened the door and poked his head inside the room.

"A word, Your Grace?" The tightness in his voice made my heart lurch. I slipped off the bed and quickly joined him in the hall, hoping I wasn't about to receive a lecture for the way I'd handled our earlier meeting with Mandy. I didn't like fighting with him, but I wasn't the type to cower either.

"Seems a little soon for an apology, but I won't complain if that's why you're here," I said, attempting to earn a smile. I hated to see him so grave.

"I wish that were the reason, my dear." He glanced over my shoulder, back toward the foyer. Then I noticed the suit he'd changed into.

"What is it?" I asked, hugging myself.

"I just received a call from Lord Carter. The council will be here at any moment to conduct your and Ursula's one-year evaluation."

I blinked stiffly. "What?"

"I thought they would go about the task at Imbolc, but I was apparently mistaken." Dante straightened his tie. "You must go to Ursula and make peace—"

The chime of the doorbell echoed through the south-wing hallway and cut off his words, but as soon as it fell silent, Dante cupped my shoulders and pressed a desperate, fleeting kiss to my lips.

"This very second," he finished. "I will not be able to

entertain or detain them forever."

Chapter Eight

I wanted to believe that Dante had come to me because he knew I was the rational one who could swallow my pride long enough to stroke Ursula's ego so she'd play nice while the council was here.

Not that I had any intention of doing that.

The princess would see right through false flattery. Besides, I was still bitter, and there were other ways to get her on board with the freakshow we were expected to put on for our critics without a rehearsal.

When Ursula wasn't in the throes of a Jekyll and Hyde meltdown, she was a reclusive bookworm. The majority of our lessons took place in the library, and that was where she spent nearly every minute of her spare time. Even more so since Lili's remark about Ursula becoming queen one day.

Either the princess was studying up on how to be a queen bee, or she was looking for a respectable way to dodge the responsibility. My guess was the latter. After all, she had volunteered to take Alexander's place at Lili's side whenever the queen was ready to depart for her forever rest. I'd taken offense at the time, but I'd kept the hurt feelings to myself.

I realized that I wasn't a conventional or classically trained blood heir, but Ursula wasn't exactly a coveted choice for a sire either—royal status aside. Her last two scions had turned out to be total heathens, setting up a seedy blood brothel that preyed on homeless girls, including Mandy.

My arrangement with Ursula had been thrust upon us, and we weren't compatible by any stretch of the imagination, but I'd really thought that we were making progress. After tasting her blood last Imbolc—and witnessing her final moments as a mortal in Morgan's loving embrace through the Eye of Blood—I had hoped we were on our way to better things. Not *lesbian* better things, but some sort of familial friendship or mutual respect, at the very least. That hope was dead now.

I found Ursula hunched over a spread of leather-bound volumes that covered one of the library tables. Most of the books were ancient with peeling spines and yellowed pages. There were dozens of them, many lying open as though Ursula were reading them all at once. Or maybe her mind was unravelling. The signs were all there, bright red flags flapping in the breeze of her stormy moods.

Her black sweater dress looked like the same one she'd been wearing the night before. Had our confrontation rattled her that badly? Or was her reading habit so intense now that it had taken a bite out of her hygiene? I couldn't decide.

Despite the recycled attire, Ursula looked decent enough for company. Her curls were darker and thicker than Laura's, but they were also natural, falling in loose waves over one shoulder. Laura had our baby-fine blond locks to work with. Nothing her fleet of hair stylists couldn't handle on set, though.

"You're a brave soul." Ursula snapped a book shut and glanced up at me, her features darkening. "Come to beg for forgiveness?"

"Would you believe me if I said yes?"

She snorted and turned her attention back to the table full of books. "I take it back. You're not brave. Simply stupid."

"The council just arrived for our one-year evaluation," I said, taking a few careful steps inside the room. "Think we could put this feud on hold long enough to pretend we're a happy family for the spectators?"

Ursula's cold gaze drew up to meet mine again. "You're lying," she accused, though it sounded more like a question.

"Do you think I'd be here otherwise?" I hitched an eyebrow. "Dante is entertaining them as we speak."

"Entertaining whom, precisely?"

"How should I know?" I snapped. "He sent me to kiss and make up with you."

Ursula's eyes finally widened with belief. She closed a few of the books on the table before barking at me. "Well, don't just stand there. Help me put these away! Do you think I want those nosy bastards poking around in my studies?"

I crossed the room to gather up an armful of books and

began tucking them away on the shelves.

"Never mind the order. Just hurry. I'll fix things later," she said, jamming a volume into a slot where the book in my outstretched hand was meant to go.

"What are you studying?" I asked, reading off the title. *Early Trials of Vampiric Legislature in the New World.*

"Mind your business, vampling." Ursula snatched the book out of my hand and shoved it into the nearest gap. "And keep your mouth shut when we meet with the council. I'll do the speaking. Say nothing."

"What if they ask me a question?"

"I will answer it on your behalf."

"That won't be suspicious at all." I put away the last book I'd grabbed and turned back to the table for more, only to be cut off by Ursula.

The manic paranoia in her gaze set my teeth on edge. I recognized the look from the lessons that occasionally deteriorated into centuries-old conspiracy theories and revenge plots that had not yet finished playing out. Vampires could hold grudges like nobody's business.

"Everything they ask will have a purpose," Ursula said through clenched teeth.

"Pretty sure that's the point." I rolled my eyes. "We're being evaluated."

"Their questions are not designed to evaluate." Ursula

grabbed my wrist as I reached past her for another book, making sure she had my full attention. "They will be carefully crafted to find any minuscule fracture they can detect within our union. Their goal is to invalidate what we have."

"And what *do* we have, Your Highness?" I asked, unable to keep the spite out of my voice. Her grip tightened, but she stopped before it became painful.

"Right now? We have a means of survival."

"So, what?" I said, struggling to keep my voice from cracking. Letting Ursula seem the more terrified one gave me leverage, and I could use more of that. "If they don't like our answers, won't they just stuff you in a coffin like you threatened to do with me?"

An annoyed growl rolled from her lips. "If I *were* to put you in a coffin, it would be for a night or two at most. To teach you a lesson. If the council doesn't like our answers, we'll *both* end up in coffins. Forever."

"Are you sure about that?" I cocked my head. "Because I really don't see what they'd have against me. I'm just a lowly vampling who ended up with you because I was in the wrong place at the wrong time."

The fear in Ursula's expression peaked and then shut off like a switch. I'd pushed too far, and my plan had backfired. The edges of the princess's psyche ended in steep cliffs that plunged into frozen darkness. Once she lost her footing, all bets were off.

"Do you suppose the council will view you as a harmless victim of circumstance if they discover who your true sire is?" Ursula asked, blinking stoically at me.

Panic rose like bile in the back of my throat, but I did my best to swallow it back. "That information is just as damning for you as it is for me."

"Perhaps." Ursula picked up the last book on the table and reached over my shoulder to put it away on the shelf. Then her empty eyes fell on me again. "But if I go down, don't think for one second that I won't take you with me."

A chill rocked my shoulders against my will, but Ursula barely seemed to notice or care in her daze. She turned and headed for the exit, gliding across the floor like a ghost. I decided maybe my plan hadn't backfired too horribly. Her deathly calm was sure to unnerve the council, as well.

I should have been relieved that only three members of the council were present to conduct the one-year evaluation. But it was the *who* rather than the number that disturbed me.

Regina Beauclair, Nicoli DeAngelo, and Louise Peyroux were waiting in the foyer with Dante when Ursula and I finally arrived to the party, stepping off the last step of the north-wing stairwell. We each took a turn to bow and offer the expected, insincere greetings.

Lady Beauclair clasped her hands eagerly in front of her navy-blue power suit. She seemed the most pleased with herself. I imagined the pop-in evaluation had been her idea. Despite the bitter cold, her cleavage peeked through the loop of a silk scarf draped around her neck, and open-toed heels revealed a glossy pedicure of white polish.

"I've heard your pending scion is musically gifted, Your Grace," she said, nodding at the baby grand set off to one side of the foyer. "Will she be joining us?"

"I'd rather not disturb the future baroness with this *unsavory* business." Dante's smile didn't waver, but the intent behind his words was crystal clear. Audrey was to be left alone. He'd tolerate their presence and let them carry out their evaluation, so long as they didn't forget whose house they were in.

Beauclair giggled, but it was less convincing this time. She turned her attention from the duke to sneer at the decorated tree in the corner. The white lights twinkled over the glossy piano lid and hardwood floor. It warmed my heart with fond memories of Midwinter. I was glad that Dante had offered no apology or excuse for our prolonged holiday decor.

Screw these Scrooges and the limo they rode in on.

Murphy and Lane stood still as toy soldiers in the mouths

of the south and north-wing hallways. I was sure there were more guards nearby—just in case. But Dante wouldn't line them up and confirm our lack of trust in the council. He would accept their judgments with as much grace as was expected of a duke, but that didn't mean he had to like it—or them.

Two men I didn't recognize, likely council guards, stood just inside the front entrance, wearing light gray suits with no ties. If any mobsters went to heaven, I was sure that this was their dress code.

Despite the muscle, Lord DeAngelo had an antsy, impatient air about him, as though he had somewhere else he'd rather be. He rubbed the stubble along his jaw as he examined the sunset prints flanking Dante's office doors, hardly sparing a sideways glance at Belinda as she handed him a saucer and cup of blood. He was dressed in a suit as well, though it was an oily black as dark and lustrous as the ponytail hanging over his shoulder.

It was no secret that Lady Beauclair and Lord DeAngelo were not fans of House Lilith. And although Lady Peyroux had voted in our favor at Ursula's trial, I was aware of her ties to House Sorano. Now that *I* was under the microscope alongside the princess, I feared my feud with Vanessa would not tilt the scales in our favor.

House Peyroux operated a botanical garden and

wolfsbane farm in Oregon. It was a more laid-back trade compared to real estate and architecture, Beauclair's and DeAngelo's chosen industries, and it showed in the casual way Lady Peyroux dressed. Her ruffled wrap dress looked as though it had come from a vintage Paris boutique—and it very well could have. Along with her vote at Ursula's trial, she had offered her sympathy by sharing how she'd lost her own sire to a Dutch assassin before fleeing France.

Despite my worries, Lady Peyroux was the most polite of our uninvited guests. Just here to do her civic duty as the head of a noble vampiric household. She sipped daintily at her cup of blood as she wandered the foyer, coming to a stop in front of the piano before gazing up at my portrait of Ursula.

"Your work, I presume?" she asked, shooting a questioning gaze over her shoulder at me.

"Yes, ma'am." I folded my hands behind my back, a leftover habit from my training at the bat cave.

"You are quite good. Do you have others on display?"

"Not yet," Ursula answered. I'd already forgotten her instruction to keep my mouth shut. "She'll be rendering a portrait of the duke and his new scion after Imbolc," Ursula added at Lady Peyroux's disappointment.

"I should like to see that when it's done," Peyroux said, her eyes flitting from the princess to me and back again as though she couldn't decide whom to address.

"Come now, Louise," Beauclair cooed sweetly. "Let us not count our chickens before they hatch. We haven't even begun our evaluation."

"We're ready when you are." Ursula forced a smile that didn't quite reach her eyes. "Where would you like to start?"

"Normally, I'd say at the beginning." Beauclair clasped her hands together, rubbing them excitedly. My insides churned as I tried to maintain a straight face. "But given current events, I'm ever so curious to know what your scion was doing working a Blood Vice investigation earlier this week."

I watched Ursula from the corner of my eye, suddenly thankful that she'd insisted on answering on my behalf. If I had to bullshit us through this one, we were doomed.

"My scion—Agent Skye—captured a known criminal." Ursula turned her cool gaze on me. "Isn't that so?"

I nodded once, still biting my tongue after my first slip-up.

Beauclair gasped, though I was sure her surprise had more to do with Ursula's shameless demeanor than the answer itself. "You knowingly allowed your scion—the Duchess of House Lilith—to engage in this reckless conduct?"

"She is a trained Blood Vice agent."

"It is quite unbecoming of a royal heir, is it not?"

DeAngelo interjected.

Ursula blinked innocently. "Is there some rule against royal scions serving in law enforcement?"

It was an admirable act, and I knew she had to be seething on the inside at having to defend the actions she'd ripped me a new one for just two nights ago. In this very room.

"I'm unaware of any such law," Peyroux confessed, earning a tight-lipped frown from Beauclair.

My pulse skipped at the admission. If the princess managed to sell them on the idea that she condoned my involvement with Blood Vice, then how could she keep me from it in the future? The thought put an ache in my cheeks as I struggled to keep from grinning like an idiot.

Maybe the council finding out about my extracurricular activities wasn't such a bad thing after all, though the *how* was still concerning. Someone in Blood Vice was obviously sharing case details with civilians—and for an ongoing investigation since Cable had vowed to uncover any additional victims of Wikes'. A double no-no.

"Our enemies have grown bold in recent years," Ursula said. *Exhibit A,* I thought, biting my tongue. "A battle-skilled scion is quite beneficial, but that benefit will run dry if her talents are allowed to rust. Besides, she was not alone in her endeavor."

"It is unconventional," DeAngelo said as if that were a

crime in itself. He tilted back his cup of blood and downed it in one swallow, then his brow puckered with disgust. The insult to our harem was duly noted. He set the cup and saucer down on the dust cover of Audrey's piano. "Many will disapprove of how far this strays from tradition." He shot a smug grin at Dante as Belinda hurried to collect the abandoned china.

"Maybe it's time to start a new tradition," the duke said, his gaze boldly holding DeAngelo's.

I'd been given the shorthand backstory of the noble households just before Ursula's trial, but something from one of the princess's tedious lessons resurfaced, a disagreement over tradition. Lord DeAngelo had not approved of Alexander choosing Dante for his first scion. He—and many others—believed the royal family should be artistically gifted.

"Well," Beauclair said, her voice downshifting, "we have other business to attend to this evening. But we shall return to launch our official inspection and take more thorough notes. Your Grace"—she smiled sweetly at Dante—"please have the entirety of your security staff and blood harem available for questioning from dusk until midnight tomorrow."

"As you wish," Dante said, then opened a hand toward the front entrance, encouraging the council to get the hell out of our home.

Chapter Nine

Ursula waited to slip back into one of her manic spells until after Dante had sent Belinda away to prepare the harem for the coming inquisition. I was certain that Murphy was already briefing the off-duty guards in his office in the basement.

"Unbecoming?" The princess seethed as she paced before the fireplace and glass wall that spanned the back of Dante's room. "What do you call dropping in unannounced and leading a witch hunt based off an event that was a success?"

"A success?" I pressed my lips together to keep from smirking. "You didn't seem to think I was so successful the other night."

Ursula stopped in front of my armchair and turned her glassy eyes and unhinged gaze on me. "Just because it was a success doesn't make it any less stupid. As you can see, it has done us no favors with the council." She stepped in closer, forcing me to crane my neck to look up at her. "They will undoubtedly count this against us in the evaluation."

"For what it is worth," Dante said, touching Ursula's shoulder to draw her attention away from me, "you did a wonderful job handling the interrogation."

"It's worth nothing." Ursula ripped her arm away from him and retreated to one side of the fireplace, glaring out across the darkened lawn as if searching for spies or assassins. She'd had more than her fair share of both, and I was sure that contributed to her...*issues.*

"How long will this evaluation take?" I asked, sticking to the facts since the what-ifs were useless stress fodder.

"A full night?" Dante shrugged. "Perhaps two. They will certainly be gone before Imbolc to prepare with their households."

"And what sort of things will they ask our donors and security?"

"Baited questions, to be sure." Ursula huffed. I could think of a few inquiries that were innocent and damning enough. Apparently, Dante could, too. He folded his arms and leaned against the fireplace mantel.

"Such as: How does the princess discipline the duchess when she is displeased with her behavior?" he asked.

Ursula's chin hitched as she turned to glare at him. "Would you have preferred me to lock her away in a coffin and leave your bed cold at dawn?"

Dante's brows rose. "Touché," he said, echoing my opinion. "And this is why we prepare our household."

"And...what?" I snorted. "Tell them to lie their asses off?"

"We give them an acceptable version of the truth," Dante said. "The princess verbally reprimands the duchess if she is not satisfied with her performance. The duchess has never left the premises without an escort."

"And everyone plays along?" I'd dealt with plenty of petty crime duos who couldn't keep a story straight between the two of them. With the guards and harem, our household was a hundred strong. "That's expecting a lot," I said.

Dante nodded. "It is. But we invite only the best into our home, and they are always well taken care of. We should count ourselves lucky that the council had other matters to tend to this night."

"It is too little time to prepare," Ursula said, absently slipping a fingernail between her teeth. She left the window and deposited herself in the empty armchair next to mine. "You've ruined us."

"Me?" I gaped at her. "I'm not the one who does all the screaming and china smashing around here—"

"If you were not such a worthless scion, I wouldn't be driven to such depraved behavior."

"Well, if your lessons weren't riddled with so much prehistoric drama, maybe I'd have a better idea of what the hell you expect from me."

"You vapid leech!" Ursula slapped the tabletop between us with enough force that I jumped. "The history of House Lilith is now *your* history as well, and if you do not study it, you are doomed to repeat it. Your ignorance endangers us all." She looked at Dante and held out her hands, palms up. "Do you see what I have to endure?"

I ground my teeth and squeezed the arms of my chair to keep from reaching over the table and strangling her.

"Please," Dante said, his brows arching. He looked at each of us, but I could tell he was pleading more with me, begging me to yield to the princess. "Let us get through this evaluation, and I will gladly take over the duchess's next history segment. You've been working too hard, Your Highness. A little rest would do you some good."

And breaking her face would do *me* some good, but I kept that insight to myself. Besides, I couldn't complain about having more time with Dante, as long as his lessons sounded less like a blood-soaked recap of a *Jersey Shore* episode. Thinking of bad television, Laura popped into my mind.

"Shit." I jolted up out of my chair. "Someone needs to check Laura into a hotel. Like, now."

"Laura?" Ursula's eyes narrowed. "Your sister out in California?"

"Uh..." I swallowed and glanced at Dante.

"I am so sorry, my dear." He closed the gap between us and took one of my hands in his. "But she cannot be permitted to leave until the council finishes their evaluation."

"What?" My voice trembled in my throat. "No, but...she has nothing to do with this."

"Mr. Murphy has already located two wolves who are watching the manor on behalf of the council. Our every move is being noted. Anything and everything we do will be dissected and used against us."

"Is someone going to explain why *my* scion has a *human* guest, and I was not told?" Ursula shrieked.

Dante closed his eyes and released my hand, pinching the bridge of his nose as he turned to answer the princess. "She has not been here long, and you have been...*reclusive*, cousin. I was considering updating you shortly before the council arrived."

"Considering." She snorted. "Is that your *acceptable version of the truth?*"

I didn't give Dante a chance to reply. "What do you care if my sister visits? I can't exactly go see *her* whenever I want to, now can I?"

"Your sister is a human celebrity." Ursula covered her face with one hand and groaned as if she couldn't believe how incredibly stupid I was. "Paparazzi tail her everywhere. Don't think I haven't seen the tabloids Mandy leaves lying around in the harem. If one of them should get a picture of the two of you—"

"It's not like I went out to get a mani-pedi with her." My jaw clenched. "That might have warranted a 'Mother, may I?' But watching television in my bedroom hardly seems like something that should require your royal blessing, Your Highness." I rolled my hand in a mocking gesture and bowed my head.

Dante's cell phone buzzed, and he held up a hand, silencing us as he fetched it from his pocket. "It is Regina." He gave us a stern look, demanding our silence, before answering the call. "How may I help you, Lady Beauclair?"

He was silent for a long moment as the councilwoman's high-pitched voice buzzed unintelligibly through the receiver at his ear. I tried to make out what she was saying—from the strain on Ursula's face, I could tell she was doing the same—though I only caught a few words, none of which made sense out of context.

"How fortunate you were not in your rooms at the time," Dante finally said, pausing to glance down at the screen of his phone. "That must be Blood Vice calling to inform me now. You are of course welcome to stay with us here in Ladue. I will have Belinda prepare three guest suites."

Ursula and I looked at one another. Her eyes reflected the same horror I felt swirling up through my stomach and into my throat. What the hell was Dante doing to us? When he ended the call, Ursula stood and faced him. Her mouth opened, but she looked too confused and hurt to think clearly. So, I spoke for both of us.

"Have you lost your fucking mind?"

Dante cringed at my crass language, but I didn't care. It was a legitimate question and deserved more than one expletive. He held up a finger, quieting me again as a new call came in.

"Captain Nicks... Yes, I am aware... I have a personal interest in this investigation. Please, keep me abreast of your findings... Very good." The call ended, and he immediately set to scrolling through his contacts.

"Dante," Ursula said, scoffing at his inattentiveness. She was used to being coddled by the duke. I found the change in him alarming, as well.

"The Nightfall Opera House is ablaze," he said, eyes still glued to his phone. "Blood Vice has not yet determined if it was arson, but the council believes it was an assault intended for them. The fire began on the floor where their rooms were located."

"Or one of them started the fire in order to score a sympathy invitation to stay here," I suggested, realizing right away how paranoid I sounded. Ursula was rubbing off on me, despite my best efforts to remain of sound mind.

"I suppose that is possible," Dante said. "But baseless accusations will get us nowhere. They are just as likely to suspect us of attempting to thwart their evaluation. Inviting them to stay here is the best way to prove our innocence."

"I don't like it." Ursula folded her arms. "Rescind the

invitation. Let them waste their time hunting for new accommodations."

"This is my house, Your Highness." Dante finally glanced up from his phone and gave Ursula a level look. "I will not go back on my word. I suggest *you* stop wasting time and help the duchess prepare the others."

Chapter Ten

This wasn't how I'd wanted to introduce Laura to my sire. Not that I'd ever really wanted to introduce them at all. They were both diva extremas, and putting two of those together in the same room was never a good idea. Especially if *my* room was being used as ground zero.

Ursula bulldozed ahead of me down the south-wing hallway, and I nearly had to run to keep up with her.

"My sister…you should know…she's—" I stammered breathlessly.

"Dead if she doesn't follow instructions."

I snatched Ursula's arm and yanked her around to face me, but she used the momentum to push me up against the wall, one hand planted on the center of my chest. My head slammed between two of Dante's sunrise prints, rattling them on their hooks, and I stumbled as I tried to stay upright.

"You dare to challenge me, vampling?" The princess's eyes filled with black as her lips stretched open, revealing elongated fangs.

"Laura's pregnant," I rasped. "Don't touch her."

I probably should have been more worried about Mandy. She'd helped me slip out of the manor undetected so we could run off and fight crime together like in the good ol' days. But Mandy was a werewolf. She had fangs of her own, and she'd survived worse than the likes of a vampy, bipolar princess.

"You are *my* scion," Ursula hissed. "Not the other way around. You will stop giving me orders as if you have a right to."

"It's not an order," I said, wheezing as Ursula pressed harder against my chest. "It's a warning."

Ursula sniffed, amused that a baby vamp like me would even think to threaten her. She released me suddenly, and I gasped in a full breath that made my head spin. The guard at the end of the hallway watched us with wide eyes, but he didn't move to help. When he noticed me staring, he turned around, giving us his back as he faced the foyer.

"I might not be as strong as you," I said, regaining my composure, "but you're relying on me to get through this evaluation, too. Don't forget that."

"As if I could." Ursula snorted and smoothed her hands down her waist to her hips. "I have no intention of harming your sister—so long as she behaves better than you do."

Not likely. I kept the thought to myself and bowed my head in gratitude.

"I will give the orders," she said. "You will make sure everyone cooperates. If they don't...you won't have a tongue to backtalk me with. Do you understand?"

I swallowed and nodded, knowing it was the best offer I'd get from the princess.

Ursula turned and continued down the hall with me close behind. Her pace was slower as if she were using the little bit of restraint she possessed to keep herself from funneling into a cyclone. I would have felt sorry for her if I weren't so terrified for everyone around us.

Ursula shoved my door open and stalked inside the room ahead of me. The television had been turned off, and only the glow of the fire hydrant lamp greeted us. The room was empty. I scanned the back wall, searching for Laura's pink luggage, but it was gone, too.

Before the relief had fully taken hold, Ursula turned on me again. In two short strides, she had my back against another wall. This time, at least, she kept her hands to herself.

"Do you think this is a game?" she asked, her eyes swirling with shadowy rage. Her mood swings were giving me whiplash.

"She was here when I left," I said, twisting my face to one side as Ursula leaned in closer, her labored breaths pelting my cheek. "Maybe Mandy took her to a hotel while we were with the council."

Usually, the princess didn't get much of a rise out of me. I'd had front-row seats to this show enough times that it was beginning to lose its thrill. But with Laura in the mix—and pregnant—I scared more easily. Which seemed to bring out the worst in Ursula. I was sure the council's close proximity didn't help matters.

"Laura's in my room," Mandy said, her silhouette darkening the doorway. "She's sleeping."

"Then wake her up," Ursula said through clenched teeth. "And what is that *horrid* stench?" She pulled away from me, and I sucked in a deep breath in preparation of her next meltdown, catching a whiff of what I suspected was the second appearance of Laura's most recent meal.

Mandy folded her arms. "*You* wake her up. I'm done getting barfed on tonight, thank you very much." She picked at a wet spot on her tee shirt and groaned. "I thought upchuck wasn't supposed to be a problem until *after* the baby arrived."

I'd told Ursula that Laura was pregnant, but at the mention of a baby, the princess's brows rose, and her mouth grew slack. She looked almost...afraid. If she hadn't believed me before, she did now. But I didn't know what to make of her reaction. Before I could give it more consideration, her mood shifted again.

"Fine. Keep her in your room," Ursula snapped at Mandy. "Representatives from the council will be staying in the guest suites across the hall, and we cannot have the duchess's uninvited human complicating matters."

"Check." Mandy gave Ursula a bored glare as she saluted with two fingers. Her wolfy ears had probably overheard the council all the way from the lobby, though their plans to bunk up with us were an extra cringe-worthy detail. This evaluation was about to get a lot more thorough than we'd counted on.

"You're to stay put, too," Ursula said to me. "No more shacking up with the duke until we get through this nightmare."

"What?" I should have expected the crackdown, but when she didn't forbid me from sleeping with Dante after my illicit outing, I'd thought we were in the clear, that maybe she'd struck some bargain with the duke that prevented her from interfering with our sleeping arrangement. "There's no rule against it," I protested. "You and Morgan were—"

"You will do as I say." Ursula's voice dropped as she stepped in closer. The eerie calm she now radiated struck more fear in me than her raving. "And from now on, you will keep my sire's name out of your hateful mouth," she said. "I will not have you abusing her memory in order to bend my will."

The thought of Dante urged me to push the issue, but Ursula was already teetering on the edge of sanity. Mandy hovered in the doorway, an anxious plea in her eyes. She would defend me with her last breath. But what sort of friend would I be if I kept putting her in situations that might require that?

"Yes, Your Highness," I answered.

"And wear something more respectable for our guests

tomorrow," Ursula added, ignoring her two-day-old dress to sneer at my jeans and knit sweater. "Perhaps one of those pantsuits you picked up in New York." She crinkled her nose, unimpressed by what I considered my nice clothes. I was just thankful that she hadn't demanded I wear a formal evening gown, though I expected to see her in one when we next met up with the council.

I tried to imagine how our first blood of the evening would go. With fancy, fanged company, I doubted the cold back patio would suffice, and three was a crowd for Dante's cozy nook in front of the fireplace.

I wondered if the duke would offer the council a bite from our harem. From the princess's etiquette lessons, I knew it was a customary favor that guests expected. Even though I wasn't supernaturally attached to any of our donors—thanks to the blood pots and lack of fang-to-flesh feeding—the idea rubbed me wrong.

Ursula's fingertips caught me under the chin, and I worried that I might have missed something she'd said, lost in my daze. She waited until my gaze met hers and then sighed.

"You are a worthy scion, as willful as you may be. We will jump through the council's hoops—together—and then work our way back toward some semblance of normal."

I blinked at her, speechless. Hopeful reassurance from the princess always caught me off guard. It was such a leap from her usual yo-yo-ing between paranoia and neurotic narcissism. I nodded before she took offense at my silence.

"I have much to think on this night," she said, more to herself than to me. "I will collect you at dusk to share my reflections before we convene with the council for first blood."

I nodded again, having nothing more useful to add. I was sure my own *reflections* would be muddled by worry and longing.

Seeming content enough with my reply, Ursula dropped my chin and swept past Mandy, turning down the hall toward her room and away from Laura. My shoulders slumped with relief. Mandy gave me a soft smile before departing, too, heading back to keep watch over my sister.

There were still a few hours until sunrise. I didn't know what to do with myself. Remembering Peyroux's interest in my portrait of the princess, I went to my drawing desk and picked up a broken bit of charcoal.

Perhaps a few new sketches would earn some brownie points. There wasn't much else to do in my room outside of watching the episode of *Henry's Courtroom* that I'd been called away from earlier. I wondered if the others had finished without me. The way Mandy balked any time I watched the show without her, it was doubtful. I decided the viewing could wait and flipped open a sketchpad.

For the first time since Dante had received the news about the opera house, I thought about Radu and the dancers who were staying at the historic venue. I hoped they were all right.

Maybe it was the fact that I so rarely got out anymore—or perhaps I was just uncultured swine who had never cared for such things as a human—but *Gelé dans la Nuit,* the winter ballet Dante had taken us to see at the Nightfall Opera House, had been magical. I'd go so far as to call it life-changing. Vampire ballerinas who'd dedicated their long lives to their craft were something special to behold.

I was willing to bet my left fang that their final show was the *other* business the council had been anxious to see to after their first pop-in. They'd dropped by just long enough to kickstart our anxiety, and then were prepared to skip off to the ballet and leave us to dwell. The fire had spoiled those plans.

A smug idea entered my mind as I put charcoal to paper. It probably wasn't a *great* idea, but would it help pass the time more enjoyably? Yes. Of that, I was sure.

Chapter Eleven

The night dragged on in solitude with only the sound of charcoal on paper to break the silence. I thought about all the things I'd done—that had been done *to* me—that the council might find fault with. Just how deeply had they dug into my life before and after my death? What did they know for certain, and what might they use to bluff damning details from us?

Shortly before sunrise, Dante slipped inside my room with a blood service tray, startling me from the deep focus of my work. My heart leapt at the thought of him spending the day in my bed—or sneaking off to his—but he stayed only long enough to steal a kiss and promise that this would all be over soon.

I drank my morning blood alone and rinsed the charcoal from my hands before turning in for the day.

As predicted, Ursula donned an evening gown the next night. What I hadn't foreseen was the blinding white color she chose. It was a blatant symbol of innocence that even *I* found a bit desperate. I'd opted for a navy Armani pantsuit and a light blue, lace-trimmed blouse. A sleek ponytail and black flats completed the look. If I'd still been a detective with Vice, I would have been the best-dressed cop in the shop.

Dante wore one of his new suits, too, though I was glad to see that he'd left his hair alone. I hated the stiff gel he often used to slick it back with for business meetings. Loose, buttery curls fell around his face tonight, and I wanted so badly to run my hands through them. It was a good thing Ursula had taken up the seat between us.

"We are between harem managers," Dante explained as Belinda circled the long table set up in the upstairs living area. The donors had been asked to stay in their rooms while we entertained the council in their space—the only place large enough to accommodate all the vamps at once. Dante was not much for entertaining, but to be fair, the queen handled most of the social activities for House Lilith.

"Have you lost another since the unfortunate incident with your pending scion's dowry girl?" DeAngelo asked, holding up his cup as Belinda stopped behind him. He reclined with one arm over the back of his chair in a casual gesture that was too comfortable for my liking.

"No," Dante answered flatly. His face gave away nothing, but his curt tone told me that he was uncertain how much the council knew about Kassandra's plotting and the reason for her current *condition*. I, too, wondered what the queen's acceptable version of the truth had included.

"Whatever happened to that traitorous little blood bag?" Beauclair asked, unwilling to pass up the opportunity to stick her nose where it didn't belong.

"She confessed," Dante said. "Answered our every question about those who coerced her into committing such atrocities."

"And where is she now?"

"I sent her away."

"Sent her away?" Beauclair scoffed. "She deserves to stand trial for her crimes."

"Her crimes were against a human in my household. What did she have to answer to the council for?" Dante blinked innocently and then nodded his thanks to Belinda as she refilled his cup.

"Was she not sent to spy on you on Kassandra's behalf?" DeAngelo asked, his eyes migrating from Dante to Ursula and then to me, searching for tells as if we were engaged in a poker game.

With the sheltered life I'd been leading at the manor, I wasn't sure how much of the truth about what had happened last fall was now common knowledge. I met DeAngelo's gaze with all the emotion of a cardboard cutout. The question had been directed at the duke, and Ursula had reminded me twice more to keep my lips zipped when she fetched me from my room earlier. I intended to do just that.

"Being ordered to do something and actually doing it are two different things, Lord DeAngelo," Dante answered. "One of Kassandra's donors murdered a girl in front of her and threatened to do the same to my sweet Audrey. She was clearly traumatized, but she did the right thing in the end."

"By killing your harem manager?" Beauclair gave him a bewildered scowl, but I could see her amusement through the ruse.

"That was a tragic accident. She fell down the south-wing stairwell." Dante straightened in his chair. "And as master of this house, I chose to handle the incident internally. I should think the council has more important matters to attend to and concern themselves with than how I operate my harem."

"Of course, Your Grace." Beauclair gave him a ruthless grin before sampling her cup of blood. Her brow puckered, and she hummed out a dejected noise. "I don't suppose you have anything...fresher?"

"Yes," DeAngelo agreed. "It's so much sweeter from the vein. I find this method utterly unappetizing—no offense, Your Grace."

Peyroux held up a hand when Dante turned to her. "I'm fine, thank you."

"Belinda," he called, drawing her attention from across the room. "Would you arrange for two live feedings for our guests?"

"Right away, Your Grace." Belinda slipped out from behind the long island that separated the kitchen from the gathering room and disappeared around the corner.

"Do you always feed in this *artificial* way, Your Highness?" Beauclair asked, clasping her hands over the table and fixing her vulturous gaze on Ursula. "Live feeding etiquette is such a vital part of a scion's upbringing, wouldn't you say?"

Ursula smiled sweetly and took a long drink from her cup, careful not to spill any blood on her white gown. She pressed her lips together and breathed deeply as if relishing every drop before she answered. "The duchess spent three months at the Blood Authority Training Center where she fed on live donors exclusively."

"Ah, yes. The bat cave." DeAngelo set down his cup and pushed it aside. "I hear you made quite a *splash* in Denver," he said, smirking at his own joke.

Shortly after arriving at the BATC, one of Scarlet's half-sired minions had locked me in a coffin and tossed me in a cave pool, passing off the attempted murder as a prank. If Roman hadn't detected me through our blood bond and alerted Kai Natani, an instructor at the base, I would probably still be there at the bottom of that pool, my lungs full of water, and my mind consumed by panic and agony.

I was sure my face was on fire from the memory, despite

my best efforts to remain neutral. DeAngelo looked all too proud of himself, but then he sucked in a sharp breath and winced.

"Oh! Apologies, my lord," Ursula said as she scooted her chair back and finished crossing her legs. "I'm not used to the extra company around the table."

DeAngelo glared at her and leaned down to rub his shin, while I bit my cheeks to keep from grinning. He didn't need to know that we never took our blood at the harem dining table. And I didn't need Ursula confessing that she'd wounded him to defend my honor. I appreciated it regardless.

Belinda returned and waited to be addressed by Dante before announcing that the donors were ready. DeAngelo and Beauclair left the table to follow her down the back hallway, and we all breathed easier with only Lady Peyroux at the table. Until she decided to pick up where the others had left off.

"I must confess," she began, allowing Dante to refill her cup, "I am quite surprised by the queen's choice of scion for you, Your Highness." She gave me an apologetic smile that was far more believable than I expected it to be. "It was curious enough when the duke allowed you to enter the Blood Vice training program as an orphaned vampling and the youngest recruit in history. But I suppose your previous training in law enforcement as a human proved advantageous, *oui?*"

I looked to Ursula, and she nodded, giving me permission to answer for myself, though her sharp gaze warned me to proceed with caution.

"Yes, my work with law enforcement as a human helped," I answered.

Peyroux nodded and took a sip of blood before placing her cup back on its saucer. "It should come as no surprise that we researched your very recent human history before composing our evaluation documents." It sounded almost like a warning that I should expect all my secrets—mortal and vampiric—to be used against me over the next few days. Where to even begin?

"Your last investigation as a human involved the Scarlet Inn, did it not?" Peyroux asked.

I took a deep breath through my nose and glanced at Ursula from the corner of one eye. She gave another subtle nod, but I could sense the way her former scion's name raised her hackles.

"It did," I said. "But I didn't know that at the time. I was just trying to free the young girls who had been abducted off the streets."

"I admire your courage." Peyroux nodded appreciatively. "But you must understand how it looked when you brought in Ursula and attended the trial that confirmed Raphael's death and saw Scarlet locked away—mere moments before replacing the pair in the royal hierarchy.”

I blinked at her, surprised by the odd turn of conversation. But then my hands curled into fists as the accusation sank in. “You think I *orchestrated* the queen naming me as the princess’s scion?”

Ursula’s hand closed over one of mine, quieting my outrage. “I think you forget how Jenna saved the queen from an assassin,” she said.

Emma Kincade, a cadet I’d trained with in Denver, had nearly succeeded in taking out the queen during the annual ceremony where Lili bestowed a drop of her royal blood to each of the new Blood Vice recruits. I’d only just recovered from the vision of the queen’s mortal death, seen through the Eye of Blood, when Emma stepped in behind me for her taste.

The House Kincade scion had pierced the queen’s heart with the ceremonial dagger and then blown silver dust into the queen’s face. It was a lethal combination—unless the lifeblood of a vampire is consumed to fast-track healing. The *blood of one’s enemy*, as the ancient texts declared. The duke had made the final call, and I’d slit Emma’s throat over Lili’s mouth, drowning out her would-be death rattle.

“Oh, I assure you, Your Highness, no one has forgotten that incident.” Lady Peyroux’s eyes narrowed on me. “It is a shame that you were not a member of House Lilith at the time. You would have been within rights to challenge the assassin to a blood duel. But you were not, and you did not. You murdered another vampire without due diligence."

"Are you suggesting that I should have let the queen die?" I snapped.

Ursula's hand tightened around my fist, but she didn't reprimand me. Her quiet words and stony gaze were all for Peyroux. "Careful, my lady. We wouldn't want the wrong person to overhear your treasonous insinuations."

The councilwoman's brown eyes filled with black. The effect was subtler than when the princess lost her cool, the contrast less jarring with her deep complexion and full, relaxed mouth. There was no snarling or hissing, no baring of fangs. Her wrath was tempered with discipline, and I immediately understood that she wasn't just a pretty face elected because she made the council look more harmless than they really were.

Dante cleared his throat, ending the staring contest between the two women. "It is regrettable that your business dealings with House Kincade have suffered, Lady Peyroux. I can understand how you might misplace that blame on the duchess."

"Do not patronize me, Your Grace." The first hint of malice entered the councilwoman's voice. "If I had any intention of misplacing blame, I would have brought up the ammunition blunder during the duchess's training that resulted in six delivery trucks being returned to Sorano Munitions. They were forced to increase production of their marker rounds to replace customer orders while their stock was being re-inspected, which meant decreasing production of the Silver Wolfsbane ammunition. They canceled their next two orders of wolfsbane from my farm."

"That wasn't my fault—" I began. Ursula squeezed my closed fist, silencing me.

"Was feeding on Vanessa Sorano's pledged scion not your fault either?"

"Agent Sorano requested a fresh harem donor," Dante put in. "I also absolved her pledged scion of the remaining years on his contract. I have more than met her demands for compensation."

Peyroux shook her head and frowned at me. "Compensation is not the council's concern. What guarantee do we have that you will not engage in such behavior again?"

"Agent Knight…he saved my life," I said, struggling with the words as thoughts of Roman entered my mind. "Twice. And I saved his."

"You were blood-bonded?" She seemed surprised by the confession. I instantly regretted telling her. "And has it faded so soon with his mortal death?"

I licked my lips and shot Dante an uncertain glance. Was

it gone? I had sensed Roman's presence when he arrived at the All Hallows' Eve ball just a few months ago. My stomach clenched, and my pulse raced whenever I thought of him now, but it wasn't a good feeling. Had it ever been?

Everyone at the table was waiting for an answer. Dante most of all.

"I have no desire to feed from him again," I said and felt a little sick at the realization that it was only true because he was no longer human.

Peyroux's expression softened with pity and skepticism. "The House Starling protégé was murdered during your training session, and the youngest member of House Novak was falsely coffin-locked."

"Both of those misfortunes lay at the feet of a half-sired member of House Hanson," Dante said, his voice rising. "You know this as well as anyone."

"So many tragic coincidences surrounding the duchess…it is disturbing, Your Grace," she said, choosing her words carefully. "But I share these concerns for your benefit, so that you might prepare for them when the others inquire."

"For which we are grateful," Dante said. I couldn't tell if he was sincere or not, though he was obviously agitated.

The plan had been for him to stay quiet and let Ursula manage on her own. She was the princess, after all, and this evaluation was for her. Not that she'd seemed terribly broken up over the intervention.

Dante held up the pot of blood, but Peyroux declined. I slid my cup across the table, forgoing etiquette as my frazzled nerves demanded more liquid courage.

The night was young, and I was already a hot mess. As Beauclair and DeAngelo returned from the harem quarters, I sent up a small prayer to whoever was listening. Then I threw back my fresh cup of blood as if it were a shot of tequila.

Ready or not, the game was on.

Chapter Twelve

DeAngelo picked up one of my latest sketches and held it under the desk light. I wondered how many centuries it had taken to perfect his look of unimpressed smugness. From my short time with him, I'd already discerned that it was his trademark expression. The corners of his mouth drooped as he took in the rest of the sketches spread over my desk and realized what my inspiration had been.

The vampiric ballerinas were fresh in my mind from Midwinter, and I'd captured them in various twirls and leaps. I didn't know the fancy names for all their moves, but that hardly mattered considering my medium. I'd gone back over the drawings with red and white grease pencils, giving them depth and a sepia-like quality.

Ursula stopped beside DeAngelo and glanced down. A faint grin lit her face as she noticed the full collection. "Handle with care, my lord. I should like to have them framed."

DeAngelo snorted and dropped the drawing he held back to my desk before heading for my open bathroom door. I hoped Laura hadn't left anything behind when she moved into Mandy's room. Prenatal vitamins and root touch-up dye would be difficult to explain to the council—and I was so very tired of all the explaining.

After leaving the harem, Ursula had led the way to the

library to show the council where she bestowed her vast, sirely knowledge upon me. They thumbed through the books and quizzed me on various topics. I was surprised to discover how much I'd learned in the past year. Of course, there were no standardized tests for fledgling scions to determine these things. I supposed the council's drilling was the next best method.

Once they were satisfied in the academic department, we took the north stairwell down to the gym. Ursula looked less sure about this part of my *training*. I let her detail how she relied on the duke's head of security to ensure that I was adequately prepared to defend myself in the outside world for whenever she allowed me to exercise my skills in law enforcement.

She went so far as to claim that the *privilege* she granted me was responsible for the capture of Kassandra's half-sired fiend—a much more useful talent than any artistic endeavors—and then offered me up for a demonstration that I was relieved the council declined. No way was I boxing Murphy while wearing Armani.

Finally, we'd ended up here, in my bedroom. With DeAngelo sneering at my drawings and Beauclair not-so-subtly running her fingertips along my furniture as if the quality of my maid service had anything to do with the evaluation. They were just prodding us now, trying to find an opening they could use to slither under our skin.

"My closet? Really?" I protested as Beauclair opened the door on the opposite side of my desk from the bathroom. She paused to give me a vicious smile.

"Is there a problem, Your Grace? Something you'd rather the council not find tucked away in here?"

"Of course not." I returned her fake expression, reining in my annoyance as Ursula shot me a warning glance. "Please, help yourself." I bit my tongue before I really screwed up and offered to give her a tour of my underwear drawer once she was done rifling through my pantsuits and nighties.

Peyroux stood by the sliding glass doors, seemingly content to let the others dig through my personal life in the most literal sense. She stared out across the lawn and up at the stars in the inky sky. The third quarter moon wouldn't rise for several hours yet, but the thin blanket of snow that covered the backyard glowed in the white lights that lined the roof. It was a lovely view that was only disrupted by the image of Mandy chasing Sweet Pea and Duncan off the terrace.

"Dogs?" Peyroux cocked her head and gave me a curious look.

"They're not mine," I said, holding up my hands. "Audrey wanted one for Midwinter. The other belongs to my...personal donor."

It was one of Mandy's technical titles, even if I hardly fed from her anymore. And she coddled Duncan enough to make the lie convincing, a stark contrast to her initial reaction to Laura's pet Chihuahua. She'd threatened to eat the dog at least a dozen times and then was suddenly in love with it.

I watched her scoop up both beasts, holding them under her arms so they couldn't reach one another. It was like watching two rabid teddy bears trying to eat each other's faces off. Mandy's mouth dropped open suddenly, and then I read her lips as she swore. A line of moisture spread down the side of her coat as Sweet Pea's bladder gave out.

DeAngelo stepped up to the glass between Peyroux and me with a shitty smirk. "Mutts are difficult enough to housebreak. Why would you bother with mortal rodents?"

"Again, not mine," I said, clenching my teeth as I forced a smile. I'd let the mutt remark go. For now.

Before Mandy had joined the St. Louis Cadaver Dogs, I'd taken more offense than she had whenever someone referred to her as a mutt. Now that she was an official member of a pack, the slur was enough to turn her eyes yellow.

I wasn't sure the insult was enough to warrant invoking a blood duel, but the Lord of House DeAngelo was an old bastard. For vampires, age came with not only knowledge but also power. It determined who could afford to be assholes and who had to watch their mouths.

"Your Grace?" Beauclair called from my closet. "What's

in this large, locked box?"

"My firearms," I answered casually, eyes still pinned to DeAngelo. Without realizing it, I'd engaged him in a staring contest. I waited for Beauclair to speak again before breaking eye contact as gracefully as I could manage.

"Should a duchess have need for such things?"

"She doesn't often," Ursula said, giving me a look that I hoped didn't mean my firepower would be moved elsewhere before the weekend was over.

"How...unsettling." Beauclair laughed dryly as she stepped out of the closet with the formal guard uniform I'd worn to Ursula's trial. It had been custom-made for me, so I hadn't thought to turn it in, and it wasn't like any of the other muscle around here could fit into it. Beauclair fingered a tear along one thigh of the catsuit.

"Bullet hole," I said, shrugging as if it were no big deal. "From the attack on the princess after the trial."

"That's it!" Beauclair's eyebrows rose, and she snapped her fingers. "I knew there was a reason you looked so familiar. You were part of the duke's royal guard—the lady escort sitting in the balcony with him."

Lady escort. That was a new one. Her tone reminded me of Lady Peyroux's insinuation that I'd orchestrated everything in order to secure my place within the royal family. My blood boiled at the idea. My only goal had been to find someone to help me through the growing pains of being a baby bloodsucker so I could carry on with my life in law enforcement. Becoming a duchess had thrown a serious monkey wrench in that plan.

"It is a shame that all three culprits were killed in battle, leaving Blood Vice no leads," DeAngelo said. He pinched the red velvet cape that shared a hanger with the catsuit, testing the quality of the material with that cocky, infuriating look of his.

"They were from the Moreau Pack—" I bit my cheek and shot a nervous glance at Ursula, wondering how much was safe to divulge to the council. Knowing something was no good if we didn't have evidence to back it up.

"Yes." Beauclair crinkled her nose. "Renegades, from the official press release. Unless you're suggesting that Marcel Moreau is more involved than he's led Blood Vice to believe?"

Questions like that were aimed to sabotage the royal family, to paint them—us—as delusional conspiracists who would abuse our authority if allowed to rule with the might we once possessed, something that had been slowly chipped away over time by greedy socialites posing as legislators.

"I wouldn't know, my lady," I said, offering Beauclair a tight smile. "I was not assigned to that case."

"Such a pity." She clucked her tongue. "While your track record is...*thin*, it seems quite remarkably complete. You don't like to leave cases unsolved, do you?"

"No, ma'am." I bowed my head slightly at what sounded as close to a compliment as I'd received from the councilwoman.

"Good." She turned and hooked my uniform over the back of my closet door. "Then, as part of your evaluation, you will solve the mystery of the Nightfall Opera House bombing."

"What?" Ursula and I asked at the same time. The princess blinked stiffly but then plastered on an insincere smile.

"I'm sure Blood Vice has already made great progress on the case," she said.

Beauclair sniffed. "They've found the charred remains of a wolf near the fire's origin, which they believe to be a bomb. On our floor."

"Perhaps it was intended for another guest?" Ursula suggested.

"Our three rooms were the only ones reserved on that level," Peyroux said, jumping on board with the idea.

I didn't particularly care who the council had pissed off enough to warrant an exploding gift basket, but working on a legit case sounded swell. It was at the top of my wish list, and it would almost undoubtedly prove that I hadn't latched on to any royal coattails for a fast-tracked ride to easy street.

"I don't see why I couldn't lend a hand?" I turned to Ursula, sensing her ire crackle like a bonfire. "That is, if it's all right with you, Your Highness?"

"This will interfere with your lessons, my dear." She huffed and scowled at the councilors, dropping the pleasant pretense. "If Jenna solves this case, you'll be satisfied with our arrangement and leave us in peace?"

"Of course." Beauclair's phony smile hadn't budged. "Provided we don't stumble upon some horrific finding during the harem and guard interviews."

"Take Agent Starsgard with you," Ursula said, grasping her hips with both hands as she turned back to me. "Levi can assume doggie duty while she's gone."

"Yes, Your Highness." I bowed to her, taking care to dip long and low for the councilors to note my respect. Then I turned to Beauclair, still standing in front of my open closet door. "Excuse me, my lady. It looks like I'll be needing those firearms tonight, after all."

Chapter Thirteen

Mandy pressed her face to the backseat window as Lane parked our car along the curb across the street from the opera house. It was almost nine o'clock, and only a Blood Vice SUV waited along the opposite curb in front of the yellow police tape that marked off the entire block.

The fire had been put out by the human fire department, though there were a couple of wolves and half-sired firemen in the mix who had made sure the local PD overlooked the sole victim—our crispy, mystery wolf.

I leaned forward to see around Mandy and took in the damage. It was worse than I'd imagined. One corner of the building, the side that held the luxury guest suites, was caved in. Uneven bricks formed a gaping maw of broken teeth that swallowed up the snow as it began to fall again.

Big, fluffy flakes filled the blackened nooks of the building and lined the sills of the arched windows—some of which were coated in soot or busted out entirely. I hated to see the opera house like this, tarnished and melancholy like a graveyard angel.

The shadows were thicker tonight, pooling against the foundation of the theater, and I realized the torch posts that lined the stairs leading up to the building's entrance were dark. It shouldn't have surprised me. There were no shows to be had tonight—or any night for some time to come.

The park lights along the sidewalk were out, too, and I wondered if the explosion had damaged the building's ancient wiring. Only the streetlamp that marked the entrance of the parking garage lit the scene. Paired with the eerie quiet, it set my nerves on edge, and my fangs scraped my bottom lip.

"I'll be waiting right here," Lane said from the driver's seat. "Got the window cracked. You just holler if you need me, ya hear?"

I could tell that he was anxious to tag along, but that would have looked bad on the evaluation. Ursula had talked me up as this competent, battle-worn hero. *Jenna Skye, Warrior Duchess*. I had to live up to that image, and besides, I had Mandy. She'd been watching my back since the night I died. I was in good hands.

I patted Lane's shoulder as Mandy opened her door. We exited the car at the same time a big man with a buzz cut and fivehead stepped out of the Blood Vice SUV. He wore a wool trench coat and stuffed his hands into the pockets as he waited for Mandy and me to cross the street.

"You the duchess?" he asked in a gruff voice as if he couldn't believe he'd been dragged out here to entertain me.

"Agent Jenna Skye," I said, ignoring his tone. "And this is my partner, Agent Mandy Starsgard."

"Captain Fred Nicks." He shook each of our hands, and

then his massive brow pinched. "Starsgard? You're one of Cable's wolves, aren't you?"

"Yes, sir." Mandy nodded.

Allen Cable was captain of the St. Louis wolf division of Blood Vice, Mandy's boss and partner whenever she ran off to fight crime without me. I couldn't help but feel a twinge of jealousy that she'd made a name for herself in the department while I'd been playing the equivalent of a royal houseplant for most of the past year.

"Yeah, Cable said your wolf can track a ghost through a thunderstorm." Nicks scratched his jaw before dipping his hand back into his coat pocket. "Wonder why he sent Ronnie out here last night instead of you."

Mandy winced. "I'm only called in for select assignments. My full-time job is with the duke's private security staff. But Ronnie is a good tracker, too."

"Huh." Nicks shrugged. "Well, you're here now. Maybe you'll catch something he missed."

He didn't have anything more to say to me, which I found odd. Vanessa Sorano had been captain during my short stint as a field agent, but I was sure Captain Nicks had seen the case file for Wikes after Mandy and I had captured him, though Cable was continuing the investigation. Even the council knew about my involvement.

Nicks turned and lifted the yellow police tape, holding it

up for us to cross under before following. We waited for him to take the lead again, climbing the stairs up to the pair of double doors on the far left. He produced a set of keys marked with an evidence tag and let us into the building.

I'd taken the time to change out of my Armani suit and into something less expensive before leaving the manor, and now I was glad for it. My boots squished in the soggy carpet of the lobby, and a smell somewhere between burnt popcorn and the scent of public restrooms permeated the air. I bit my tongue until the pain triggered my blood vision, and my breath billowed in front of my face like pink fog. I imagined the furnace had been shut down for inspection—along with everything else.

"Only brought one flashlight," Nicks said, fishing it out of his pocket. "Don't suppose that's a problem for a wolf, but you'll want to stick close and watch your step anyway. Got an inspection scheduled for tomorrow to determine structural soundness before Radu begins planning repairs."

Nicks flashed the light in my face, but it was just another wash of red in the backdrop created by the Eye of Blood. When I didn't flinch or hide behind an arm, he turned the spotlight toward the stone staircase in the far corner that led up to the guest suites.

Mandy nudged me ahead of her and took up the rear as we navigated four flights of stairs to the top level of the building. Damp soot clung to the walls. In some places, the wallpaper had blistered and peeled away from the plaster. Each floor revealed worse damage—from charred crown molding and doorframes to soot-caked brickwork and plumbing pipes exposed in places where the walls had turned to ash and washed away.

The farther we ventured, the colder it got, and once we reached our destination, it was obvious why. The gaping hole visible from outside showed where the suite's ceiling used to be in the room where the bomb had gone off.

My blood vision winked out, but I could see well enough with the stars sparkling through the demolition skylight. Not that it was much use when the rest of the room was a black hole of soot and debris. The body and all other evidence had long since been taken away to protect it from the elements and prying human eyes.

"Ronnie could tell that the vic was a wolf," Nicks said, more to Mandy than to me. "But we didn't get a hit on the DNA. Guess the guy didn't have a record. Not much to go on if we don't even know who he is."

"What kind of bomb did he use?" I asked, dusting a snowflake from my cheek.

"Homemade IED. Probably a pressure cooker or a pipe bomb. The lab is still testing the evidence we gathered," Nicks answered without looking at me. "Maybe they'll find something more than we have so far."

"I'm going to slip around the corner and shift real quick," Mandy said, shrugging out of her coat as she stepped back into the hall. Nicks nodded, though he looked uncomfortable at the idea of being left alone with me. I supposed that would make it harder to keep giving me the brush-off.

"Any security footage?" I asked, nudging my boot under a broken spindle that had likely been part of a headboard before the blast.

"You think I'd be here right now if we had anything that useful?" Nicks snorted. "Old Radu didn't want to compromise the building's historical integrity or his guests' privacy by having cameras installed. We have some footage from the parking garage across the street, but plenty of humans who work in the area like to park there, too."

"Did Radu give you access to the guest log?"

"Yeah, yeah." Nicks finally looked at me. An annoyed scowl screwed up his face, and he yanked his free hand out of his pocket to tick off the standard checklist. "We talked to all the guests, and we talked to all the employees, and the parking garage footage was put through facial recognition to check for enemies of the council. We know what we're doing, Your Grace."

I bit my bottom lip and sighed. "I suppose my politeness isn't doing either of us any favors. What I meant to say,

Captain Nicks, is that I'll be needing the guest log and staff schedule. The garage footage, too."

His nostrils flared, and his jaw flexed. For a moment, I thought he might refuse. "It's in my glove box," he said. "I'll turn it over after your partner is finished."

I couldn't understand why he sounded so butt-hurt about it until I remembered how new he was in his position as captain. He thought I was here on behalf of the duke to double-check his work.

"I'm sure you and the entire St. Louis field office have done everything by the book—"

I paused as Mandy joined us in her four-legged form. She politely ignored our conversation and put her nose to the floor, beginning on the least demolished side of the room. Her paws padded cautiously over the debris.

"I'm not here to make you look bad," I said to Nicks. "The council requested my involvement."

Probably to summon up another black mark for the evaluation. I was sure of that now, given the slim evidence we had to work with.

Nicks snorted. "Did the council request your involvement with the Wikes case, too?"

"No. I had a personal interest in that one." I cocked my head and frowned at him. "And it was one of the human PD's cold cases. Why are *your* panties in a twist over it?"

"It should have been a Blood Vice case," he snapped. "The girl's labs showing she had lycanthropy should have been flagged. And you should have reported it to Blood Vice as soon as you discovered the oversight."

"That's a lot of *shoulds*, but I'm only responsible for the last one." I shrugged. "And, technically, it is a Blood Vice case."

"*Now* it is." Nicks rolled his eyes.

"It was all along. I used Blood Vice resources. I still have my badge and was never officially fired."

"Is that so?" The captain's back straightened with the news. "Well, in that case, you're fired. Officially."

Mandy's sniffing stopped, and she lifted her head to glare across the room. Her dark fur blended with the soot-stained walls, giving her yellow eyes an extra-haunting glow. I bobbed my chin, signaling for her to go back to work. I could handle Nicks.

"Are you sure that's a good idea?" I asked, giving him a lopsided grin. "Do you really want to forfeit *all* credit for ending Wikes' reign of terror?"

"I could've settled for giving you an 'attagirl' after Wikes," Nicks said. "You're right. It wasn't even our cold case. But muddling around in active Blood Vice investigations is a whole 'nother can of worms—"

"That I wouldn't be opening if the council didn't have me

by the short and curlies." I sighed and turned away from him to accept what looked to be a scrap of torched cardboard from Mandy's jaws. "What's this?" I asked, forgetting that she couldn't answer in her wolfy form. She snorted and went back to searching the room.

Nicks pulled a white handkerchief out of the breast pocket of his coat and held it out to me. I turned over the new find without a fuss. I needed him on my side. If the lab guys found something useful, playing nice with the captain was the only way I'd be getting a heads up. Though, from everything I'd gathered so far, this case was well on its way to becoming another cold one.

"Looks like it could've been a postcard." Nicks wiped one corner of the handkerchief over the chunk of cardstock, smearing the wet soot until he could make sense of the words and imagery behind it. "There're some mountains and what looks like...*mile hig?*"

"That's gotta be the Mile High City," I said. "Denver. Maybe we should check in with their field office."

"I'll take care of that." The captain flashed me a sharp smile that didn't match his loathing gaze. "Since you no longer have clearance to receive case-related information."

"Super. That'll save me some time." I returned his smile without missing a beat. "I'm sure the duke will keep me posted if you learn anything new."

Mandy finished her loop around the room and sneezed, blowing a cloud of dark dust up from the floor. Nicks grumbled and stepped out into the hallway to wrap up the new piece of evidence and stash it inside his pocket for safekeeping.

While his back was turned, Mandy tapped her paw on another find—a small bundle of folded paper that was halfway through its metamorphosis of becoming a lump of charcoal. I knelt and pretended to tie my boot as I pocketed the crumbling sheaf.

"Are we done here?" Nicks asked as he rejoined us.

"Yup." I stood and turned to face him. "Hand over the loot in your glove box, and we'll get out of your hair."

"Works for me." He snorted and aimed his flashlight toward the stairs before marching off ahead of us. Mandy trotted off in the other direction to find her clothes and shift, while I waited impatiently for her in the mouth of the destroyed suite.

The sooner I combed through everything Nicks had, the sooner I'd be able to get the *council* out of *my* hair. If I managed to find anything useful.

It was a big *if*, but my life seemed to hang on a lot of those.

Chapter Fourteen

One of the library tables would have been a great place to go over the case documents, but according to Levi, Ursula was already losing her mind over Lady Beauclair's fondness for the duke's book collection. I would have even settled for my desk or bed, but my room had been invaded, too.

Obnoxious bickering filtered through the bathroom door. Audrey was getting a little too comfortable bossing Mandy around, but to be fair, Mandy was also part of the household security staff. She would have to be more careful about how she addressed Audrey once the girl was turned and officially named the Baroness of House Lilith.

"Your boy toy can take that...*thing* outside from now on," Mandy said. "It pissed all over my new coat."

"Boy toy? Thing?" Audrey gasped. Her Southern drawl dripped with offense, but it wasn't all for Mandy. "The last time Levi left my side, that awful Lord DeAngelo made a pass at me. Can you believe the duke asked me to play Mozart for him?"

"Then go outside *with* Levi, or stay in your room," Mandy said. "I am not your dog sitter."

"But...you've been taking Miss Laura's dog out. And Levi happily managed the task while you were away. Don't you think you should return the favor and give him a break?"

"Duncan Punkin doesn't have a bladder the size of a pea. He doesn't have to go out every half hour, and he didn't ruin my coat. Besides, I'm busy doing *real* work right now."

Laura heaved a dramatic sigh. I imagined she was still sprawled across my bed where she'd been when I'd finally had enough and retreated into the bathroom. Mandy had snuck her over for a visit, but she was only interested in asking all the questions I didn't have answers to.

How long will the council be here? When can I leave to go shopping? Is the water the harem serves pH balanced? Does this new cruelty-free, organic hair dye look too orange?

"I'll take the damn dogs out," Laura declared.

The room exploded with chatter as all three women tried to speak at once. Meanwhile, I used the toe of my boot to wedge a rolled-up towel more snugly under the bathroom door, hoping to quiet the racket.

Luckily, I'd snagged Mandy's phone before the lockdown. I cradled it between my shoulder and ear and flipped through the employee schedule for the tenth time as I waited for Dr. Delph's reply on the other end of the line.

Spero Heights' beloved shrink had given me plenty of sound advice last year—not that I'd taken any of it. I wouldn't be making that mistake again.

"I'm afraid it doesn't work that way, Your Grace," he said, crushing my hopes and dreams.

"Come on, doc. Give me something," I begged. "A name, a place. I'll take whatever you got. I *have* to solve this one. Failure is not an option."

"My visions are rooted in the affairs of my community," he said. I could almost see him shrug through the phone. "And my telepathy is close-range, as well. Beyond that, I'm a humble therapist."

"Great. Another dead end." I threw the employee schedule back onto the pile and hunched over so I could rest my elbows on the counter. My feet were killing me from all the anxious pacing I'd done between the shower and toilet.

Delph sighed. "Your detective skills have brought you this far in life, have they not?"

"You mean the detective skills that got me killed in the first place?" A nervous laugh escaped on the tail-end of my next breath. "Sure, I guess you could say that."

"Okay. Perhaps it is not skill but rather *luck* that you have in abundance."

"I'm not feeling very lucky right now, doc. The thought of getting locked in a coffin isn't doing much for me either."

"You are always welcome here, Jenna," he said. "Mayor Pierce is quite close with the duke. You would be safe."

It was a generous offer, considering how *selective* Spero Heights could be about their residents. But giving up and hiding out in a podunk mountain town of supernaturals who were even more defective than I was, was not how I wanted my story to end.

"Still experiencing conflicted feelings about your new kin?" Dr. Delph asked.

"I thought your mindreading mojo didn't work long-distance."

"I don't need to be psychic to sense the fear in your silence."

"Hmm." It was a noncommittal sound that I hoped he took for the warning that it was. I hadn't called him for help dealing with my hang-ups—as if those would matter if I ended up in a box.

"You are stressed," he said. *How very clairvoyant.* "What are you doing for self-care?"

"Uh...staying alive?" I snorted.

"It is hard to perform at our best when we fail to tend to our emotional and bodily needs."

"I've had more than enough blood tonight," I said. It was technically true. I wouldn't be shriveling up and blowing away, but with three additional mouths to feed, and the vamp guards working overtime, the harem was spread a little thin. We hadn't resorted to rations yet, but the prospect didn't seem far off.

"And your emotional needs?" Dr. Delph prompted.

I thought of Dante and how I'd be spending yet another

day without him, alone in my own bed. The council needed to go. Now. But the only way that would happen was if I figured out who had tried to blow them to the moon and back.

I glanced down at the mess crowding my sink. The employee schedule. The guest log. The crunchy, mostly burnt sheets of paper Mandy had found which contained a few useless, random words in feminine handwriting.

It wasn't enough. I needed more to work with.

"Jenna?" Dr. Delph said as if he feared I'd hung up.

"I'm here."

"Are your emotional needs being met?"

"I'm working on it."

When I finally emerged from the bathroom with the case file stuffed under my arm, Audrey was gone, and only Mandy and Laura looked up from my bed to greet me. Duncan was curled in a ball between them, snoozing despite Mandy playing with his ears and whiskers.

The tablet I'd loaded the parking garage footage onto lay abandoned in her lap, the feed still running. I nodded at it.

"Notice anything new we missed the first time?" I asked.

Mandy pressed her lips together and shook her head.

"What about you? Any earth-shattering revelations rise up from the ash of the pages I found?"

"Hardly enough letters to fill a Scrabble rack. Although, I did see a couple of Xs and Os near the bottom of one page. Maybe it's a love letter?"

"I'm hungry," Laura groaned, clearly bored with our shop talk. "I hope they send that cute Alaskan guy down with dinner soon."

"I hope he *is* dinner," I said under my breath. My mouth felt dry, and my nerves were shot.

Laura crinkled her nose. "Is it *weird* that I'm crushing on a kept man? I mean, it's not really something ladies put on their manhunting wish list, is it?"

"Should you be manhunting at all in your condition?" I asked, my eyes darting to her still-flat stomach. Her eyes followed, and she smoothed a hand down the front of her blouse.

"I won't be showing for a while, and…hello? Modern woman here. Just because I'm knocked up doesn't mean my sex life has to be over."

"Ewww." Mandy made a face, and Laura promptly smothered it with a pillow.

"Give me the tablet before you break it," I snapped, interrupting their playful scuffle and waking Duncan. The tiny dog's head wobbled unsteadily as he squinted up at me and yawned.

I hated how angry I sounded, but I felt like I was the only one taking the situation seriously. Of course I wanted to enjoy Laura's visit and daydream about the future, but there would be no future if I didn't solve this case first. At least, none for me.

Mandy turned the tablet over with a sheepish pout. "Sorry."

"No, I'm sorry," I said, tucking the device under my arm with the case file before running my hand over my face. "This is getting us nowhere. I need to check in with Ursula."

"I'll go with you," Mandy volunteered.

I shook my head. "Stay with Laura. Take care of Duncan and keep your ears pricked for the council."

"When will you be back?" Laura asked, dragging Duncan into her lap. "I've hardly seen you since those crusty old vamps showed up."

"I won't be any later than sunrise." I gave her a pained smile and headed for the door.

As much as I loved Laura, I really hoped that she was back in Mandy's room when I returned. The council was bound to come knocking for answers soon, and the last thing I needed was for my sister to add a heap of new questions to the mix. Knowing Laura, she'd go into Anastasia van de Velde-mode and sabotage whatever brownie points a closed case might earn.

I stole a quick glance down the hall in either direction before exiting my room and making a beeline for Ursula's. Her door was a short distance from mine, but the guest suites were just across the hall, and I wasn't ready to admit that I had zero news for the council.

I didn't bother knocking as I entered the princess's room and found Dante sitting in the corner lounge chair, an espresso cup in one hand, and a saucer in his other. Ursula faced the sliding glass doors that led out to the terrace. She still wore her white gown from earlier in the evening.

"Jenna," Dante said, guilty surprise pinching his expression as he stood. "I was just on my way to see you."

"Really? But you look so cozy."

"Your room…it sounded…congested."

"That's no joke."

"I did not wish to interrupt." He smiled weakly at his excuse as if it sounded spineless even to him.

I dropped the case file and tablet on the corner of Ursula's bed and folded my arms. "There's nothing here. I need more information if I'm going to solve this case."

"You have everything Captain Nicks was given," Dante said.

"Minus the interviews Blood Vice conducted—which I don't want anyway. I'd like to conduct my own."

"That can be arranged." Dante set his cup and saucer down on the table beside the lounge chair and dug out his phone. "I'll have Nicks gather them at the precinct tomorrow evening—"

"Tonight," I said.

"But it's after midnight, my dear." His brows drew up in the center, and he pressed his lips together. The gentle look usually turned me to pudding, but I resisted this time.

"Then I'll start with Radu. We know where to find him, right?"

"You can't be serious."

"As a fresh grave."

"It's out of the question," Dante said.

"Then I guess it's a good thing I didn't ask you." I turned to Ursula. "You're my sire. How soon do want this case solved and Lady Butt Hair on her way home?"

She stared blankly for a few seconds before realizing that I meant Beauclair. Dante had already covered his face with one hand, though I wasn't sure if it was to hide his amusement or frustration. Maybe both.

"It is a little *congested* around here, isn't it?" Ursula held a hand out at Dante, palm up. "I'm tired of drinking blood from china all the time. I want something—some*one*—I can sink my teeth into."

"Wait, you want to come with me?" I blinked at her,

dumbfounded.

Ursula gave me a dark look. I could tell she was trying to be annoyed, but there was a spark of intrigue swirling in her eyes. She'd been hiding under a rock long before I helped put her under Dante's thumb. I supposed she could use a girls' night out more than anyone.

"You are the Princess of House Lilith," Dante said, his voice rising. "You cannot be seen prowling a blood club—certainly not while the council is overstaying their welcome."

Ursula flicked her fingers dismissively. "We will take guards with us, of course."

Dante huffed and turned his desperate face to me. His mouth worked, but no words came out. He knew as well as I did that Ursula was even less inclined to listen to me. But for once, the princess and I were on the same side.

Chapter Fifteen

Ursula's breath fogged the window as she took in the city lights. She hadn't been this nervous about our trip to New York City to watch the ball drop, but Dante had rented a private, skyrise suite for us away from human eyes. He'd also brought harem donors. Walking through a throng of sweaty bodies and supping on a stranger was quite a different story.

The glittery, emerald dress she'd chosen was more suited for the red carpet than a nightclub, but Ursula didn't own any fishnets or latex. She didn't have anything even remotely punk, and her version of Gothic was a bit of a stretch from the modern usage of the word. I supposed, as the princess, she'd wow the masses regardless of what she wore.

I quit offering suggestions when she asked if I truly planned to dress like a streetwalker. My leather pants and cropped, lace blouse was the most modest ensemble I'd outfitted myself in for Bleeders.

"Is it always this crowded?" Ursula asked, taking in the packed parking lot and the long procession of cars dropping off patrons near the unmarked entrance.

I shrugged. "I've only been here a handful of times, but I'm guessing there are fewer options at the moment."

"Yes, I suppose so." Ursula's brow creased as Murphy looped around the backside of the lot to find a parking space.

"You don't have to do this—"

"I don't need your permission to be a coward, vampling. We both have need to be here tonight, and I intend to satisfy mine. Fully."

Murphy pulled the car in at an odd angle, taking up two full spots under a security light. Then he twisted around in his seat to get a good look at us. "The boss said I'm to pat down anyone you decide you wanna take a bite out of, Your Highness. Unplanned outing or not, we can't take any chances with your safety."

He was even more uptight than Dante had been, but that might've had something to do with the satiny gold suit Ursula had picked out for him. Lane wore a matching one where he sat in the front passenger seat. I'd caught him admiring himself in the side-view mirror more than once on the way to Bleeders.

"I'm not here for the snacks," I said, patting Murphy's arm where it rested over the divider wall between the front and back seats. "I just need to ask Radu a few questions. I won't be long."

"Take your time," Ursula said, her gaze sliding away from Murphy to trail after a lanky woman with rainbow dreadlocks and flashing platform heels. The lady walked toward the line outside Bleeders' entrance with a small crowd of friends.

"We won't be standing out in the open with the civilians

either," Murphy said, frowning ahead of the woman. "The boss called ahead. Radu is expecting us."

"Super." Ursula licked her lips. "What are we waiting for?"

Murphy inhaled slowly and gave me a reprimanding scowl. He thought this bad idea was all mine, but I couldn't tell him that he was only half right. Not with the princess looking like the cat about to eat the canary—*canaries*, I amended as she eyeballed another colorful patron lining up outside. Murphy finally nodded to Lane, and the guard climbed out of the car with a spring in his step.

"Showtime," he said in an excited voice as he opened my door.

Ursula put a hand on the back of my shoulder, letting me pull her across the seat as I exited the vehicle. Her sparkly dress was snug, and she was therefore not overly mobile. But I guessed that was the way they did things in the merry o' land of Oz. Once out of the car, she took Lane's arm. They were a matching pair, and both seemed eager to see where the night might lead.

Murphy, on the other hand, looked like he'd rather hide in poison ivy-choked bushes than be seen dressed like a Vegas show host. He didn't offer me his arm either, for which I was grateful. I liked keeping my hands free, even if the only weapon I'd be able to smuggle in was the silver-pronged stun gun I'd used on Wikes. It was better than nothing.

"Are you sure you're safe with Radu Vlad?" Murphy asked under his breath as we neared the front door.

"Safe enough. You should stay with the princess. Don't let her get carried away."

He snorted. "Easier said than done."

A few curious eyes migrated toward us as we strolled past the long line. A couple of patrons grumbled, but then someone recognized Ursula.

"Look! It's the new princess!"

"Do you think she's thirsty?"

"I hope she drinks my blood!"

A small smile pulled up one side of my mouth when I realized that no one seemed to recognize me. Maybe it was the full black ensemble. Or perhaps no one expected to see me here again after the last time. Zane, Radu's pretend scion, certainly seemed surprised when the doorman ushered us inside.

"Radu said you were on your way, but I still can't believe my eyes." He shook his head and then bowed—mostly to Ursula—before nodding for the doorman to run his metal detector wand over us. When it went off near my front pocket, I pulled out a thick, leather sleeve.

"Phone case," I explained, hoping they wouldn't ask me to open it.

Zane motioned for the guard to scan my midsection again while I held the case. Another guard gave us each a black bracelet to denote our fanged status. Ursula fingered hers as we moved away from the front of the house and followed Zane through to the heart of the club. Then she glanced around the room at the different wristbands worn by the customers.

"Black means vamp, and red means available donor," I shouted to be heard over the music that pumped like a racing pulse in time with the strobe lights overhead.

"Then why is this morsel wearing a black one?" She nodded at Zane's backside, and I tapped a finger over my lips, begging her to keep that tidbit to herself. I'd explain Count Denturla later. "And the other colors?" she asked, eyeing a woman in a Captain Marvel costume who was off-limits from the white bracelet on her wrist.

"White means they belong to a private harem, and yellow means they're a novice—I'd play it safe and avoid them."

"Hmm." Ursula frowned at my recommendation, but her mood shifted again as we reached the feeding booths, and the smell of fresh blood and sugary, tropical juices engulfed us. In between the thumps of bass, the sound of soft moans and wet suckling tickled my ears. The curtains were pulled closed, but the mirrors overhead revealed the tangle of bodies writhing in ecstasy just out of reach.

"Sweet bride of Dracula." Lane's fangs budded. He closed his eyes and sucked in a deep breath. "I just had a bite before we left the house. Why am I suddenly so ravenous?"

Murphy elbowed him in the ribs. "No drinking on the job."

"Yeah, yeah. I'm no dummy." Lane rolled his shoulders and straightened the lapels of his jacket. "Guess you'll know where to find me on my next night off—not that I'll want you to."

Zane led us past the juice bar in back where most of the red bracelet-wearing patrons who didn't currently have fangs in them waited, sipping on fresh-squeezed cocktails and making eyes at the vamps. Ursula stared longingly at them over her shoulder as we headed to the elevator tucked in the corner.

"I have no business to discuss with Vlad." She propped her hands on her hips and huffed at Zane. "Unless there are more warm bodies upstairs, I'd prefer to wait down here."

"Of course, Your Highness." He bowed again and dug a handful of free drink tokens out of his pocket, quickly handing them off to Murphy. "Please, enjoy."

"You know how it works here, right?" I asked Murphy, hoping to spare the princess from the same embarrassment I'd endured my first time. For one-night donors, the currency was overpriced juice—at Bleeders anyway. Offering money was offensive. It violated some nonsensical code of ethics that no one but the regulars seemed to understand.

"I've been here before," Murphy admitted. The blush in his cheeks told me that he'd had an equally novice experience.

"I'll be as quick as I can," I promised. Murphy nodded and turned to follow Ursula and Lane back to the bar.

The elevator doors slid open, and Zane placed a hand on the inside frame, holding it open. "After you, Your Grace." The title sounded sardonic coming from his lips, as if he didn't believe I deserved it. I wasn't so sure I did either, but giving it back wasn't really an option.

"That's *Agent* Your Grace, to you," I said, stepping inside the elevator. He joined me with a smug grin.

"Thought we'd seen the last of you after the queen's adoption. Just can't stay away, huh?"

"Must be your magnetic personality that keeps me coming back."

"Or maybe you're looking to settle a score?" He raised an eyebrow, and his gaze darted down at my pocket. "Radu asked that I not insult the princess by suggesting that her scion was trying to sneak in a weapon, but you've fooled no one."

I shrugged. "Don't worry. It's not for you, lover boy."

The elevator opened on the top floor, the one that held Radu's surveillance office and his swanky loft apartment. Though I hadn't expected any trouble, I was still relieved not to be on the floor below, a labyrinthine, concrete nightmare, reflecting Bleeders' violent reputation that kept customers in line.

Zane led me past a long window that revealed the security team who monitored all video feeds from cameras inside and outside of the building. An industrial nightclub could not boast the rich history of the opera house, but that also meant that Radu had no problem dolling it up with all the modern gadgets he could get his hands on.

The boss vamp's apartment was right across the hall from the video room. Zane knocked, and a beefy guard let us in. Three more waited inside, all gathered around a long folding table lined with business ledgers and binders full of water-damaged documents. Extension cords stretched across the hardwood floor, connected to the blow-dryers the men wielded. Zane left my side to join them in their task.

"Jenna!" Radu called from the piano in the corner. He crossed the room to take my hand in one of his, dropping a kiss on my knuckles as if we were old friends. In his other hand, he held a whiskey glass full of dark blood. Several more were scattered around the long table between books and dryers. Something to soothe the egos of the guards he'd recruited to dry out his soggy collection.

"From the opera house, I take it?" I cocked my head at the mess.

"I'm afraid so." Radu sighed. "How goes the investigation?"

"Well…" I didn't guard my hopeless expression quickly enough.

"That bad, is it?" He clicked his tongue and downed the rest of his beverage before turning back toward the piano. A crystal decanter of crimson liquid rested on a serving tray atop the baby grand, along with a silk smoking jacket that I guessed he'd shed thanks to the suffocating temperature in the room. "Would you like a drink?"

"I'd love one." I was already wondering how much sucking up I'd have to do to get my name scratched off Bleeders' blacklist. If I couldn't get rid of the council soon, I would have to figure something out. Anemic Jenna was no fun.

"The duke tells me that the council assigned you to this mystery." Radu turned over a fresh glass and filled it before replenishing his own.

"They think the bomb was intended for them," I said.

"I would not be so certain."

"Did you have another high-profile guest that Captain Nicks' guys overlooked?"

Radu's smile was gentle but disparaging as he returned and handed me the glass of blood. "The duke shelters you too much. Admirable when in love, but useless in the real world."

I wanted to agree with him, but saying it out loud felt too disloyal. Instead, I tipped my glass in gratitude and drank the blood in one swallow.

The heat dropped into my chest instantly and puddled as if it were melting my heart. At the same time, it sent a chill through my shoulders. I licked the corners of my mouth and tried to think of a tactful way to ask Radu if he'd spiked my drink.

"Distilled diabetic," he said, answering before I could inquire. He toasted his glass at me and took a more careful sip than I had, enjoying it the way an old fogey enjoys bourbon— neat and slow. I guessed I was playing the shot-slinging co-ed at the club tonight.

"Okay." I took a deep breath, trying to clear my head. "If you would, kind sir, un-shelter me."

Radu's amused grin faltered. "Have you heard of the Free Blooders?" When I shook my head, he went on. "They're a small but growing group of extremists and thugs. Their goal is to dismantle undead society, to overthrow the Vampiric High Council and the royal family."

"That all sounds like a good reason to attack the visiting council members."

"Maybe so." Radu bobbed his head from side to side. "But considering that the Free Blooders have been soliciting me to join their campaign, I am sure you can see why I would suspect that this attack was directed at me."

"Not really." I gave him an apologetic shrug. "They can't really think that blowing up one of your venues is a good way to get you on their side, can they?"

"The Free Blooders are not fond of the opera house. It caters to the wealthier vampiric households, many of which hold seats on the council. I think they will claim the destruction when they next contact me and threaten more of the same. I also fear they will use the increased traffic here at Bleeders to slip in undetected and recruit the younger, more impressionable vampires for their cause."

"Hmm." I nodded, having nothing more useful to add to the conversation. The hum of the blow-dryers drew my attention back to the table. "The *why* is plenty important, but for now, I'd like to focus on the *how*."

"Nicks didn't give you the interview notes?" Radu snorted. "No, of course he did not. I think I like him even less than his predecessor."

"He hasn't pushed me to that point yet," I said. It would take an awful lot to put him on par with Vanessa Sorano in my book.

Radu grumbled under his breath. "Give him time."

"From what I *do* know, the wolf who set off the blast had to have hauled in quite a bit of material to make the bomb. How likely is it that the clerks working the front desk wouldn't have noticed anything at all?"

"It is curious," Radu agreed. "But I questioned them all myself, as well. I believe they are telling the truth."

"Are there any other entrances a guest might have come in through? On the side or at the back?"

"There is a side door that offers access to the elevators. It is locked from the outside, exit only."

"Maybe he could have propped it open with something?"

Radu scratched his chin and took another drink of blood. "Yes, I suppose it's possible. Though as cold as it's been, the girls up front would have surely noticed such a draft."

"Does anyone else have a key?" I asked.

"Only the maids. An hour later, and we might have had more than one toasted wolf."

"Your maids are wolves?"

"Yes, of course. The ladies usually arrive a few hours before sunrise to ensure that our guests have clean towels and fresh sheets—anything they might need before turning in for the day. Then they clean the public spaces of the opera house after sunrise."

It made sense, but the wolf connection still nagged at me. "Did Nicks interview the maids?"

"He had no reason to." Radu waved a hand dismissively and finished his blood. "I called and told the girls not to come in."

"Do you have a schedule or list of who *would* have come in that morning?" I asked.

Radu cradled his empty glass to his chest and turned toward the table of documents. A stack of thoroughly dried binders caught his attention, and he shuffled through them until he found the one he was looking for. After thumbing through the pages for a moment, he turned the book around for me to see.

"Wanda, Heather, and Tracy were scheduled for Saturday morning," he said, tapping a finger on the list of names. Their applications are in there, too. Go ahead." He handed the binder off to me and took my empty glass. "Another?"

"I better not." My head was still spinning from the first glass. And I'd thought bloodnog was potent.

I flipped through the applications, handling the brittle, ink-blurred pages with care. They were still legible for the most part, which was fortunate since I recognized the handwriting on Tracy's.

"Tracy Young," I read aloud. "Moved here from Denver three years ago. She was scheduled to work?"

"Yes." Radu set our empty glasses down on the table and glanced over my shoulder. "Is there something I should know about her?"

"Not sure yet, but I'd like to find out." I pointed at the address listed on her application. "Still current?"

"I believe so."

"Then if you'll excuse me, I have another interview to conduct. Thanks for the blood and schooling."

On a good night, the average vamp was content with a single feeding. Just a pint of blood, the equivalent of a bagged unit, like the ones I used to drink before assimilating to this new lifestyle. Only vampires who could afford to support a large harem—or those who were staving off imminent death—drank more.

The blood pots at the manor each held a unit's worth. I often split one with Dante in the evening when we rose. Then again around midnight, and a third just before sunrise. We were never morbidly indulgent, and the only time I'd required more had been during my training in Denver when Faye Sorano, Vanessa's sire, had run me ragged from sundown to sunup.

Spacing meals out not only kept cravings at bay, it also prevented the aggressive rush of adrenaline that often followed a large feeding and saved us from acting like the monsters I still considered most of our kind. So, when Lane met me as I stepped out of the elevator and shared that Ursula was chowing down on her fifth patron, I was beyond alarmed.

"They're practically lining up outside her booth," Lane said, digging a finger over the knot of his tie to loosen it. Disco ball lights peppered his face, illuminating the film of sweat that coated his brow. "Murphy even told them the princess was out of drink tokens, but they don't seem to care. They're giving it up for free just to have the royal fang treatment."

"Great." I grimaced as I caught sight of the growing crowd of ladies. Ursula's preference was no secret, and as a royal scion, she was like the Taylor Swift of the vampire world. She'd dropped off-grid for a while, but now she was back with a vengeance.

"We need to get her out of here," Lane shouted over the music. "This is turning into too much of a security risk."

"Lead the way."

I hooked a hand over his shoulder as he turned around and let him drag me through the crush of sweaty bodies swarming the dance floor. They spilled into the narrow aisle that circled the room and ran in front of the feeding booths. I glanced up at the mirror over Ursula's enclosed nook.

Clubbers filled the cubicles on either side of the princess. Some stood on the cushioned benches, their arms waving over the dividers, shaking their red wristbands for her to see that they were available and willing. I remembered how Vin had been that desperate for me to feed from him. The memory made my skin crawl.

Adrenaline junkies did not make for good blood donors. I supposed that was why so many of them hung around clubs like Bleeders instead of being recruited for legit harems.

As Lane and I neared the booth, the mass of bodies became harder to squeeze through. I had to shoulder-check a few customers to get their attention so they'd move. Some still hesitated until they saw my black wristband and the feral look in my eyes.

I hadn't been big on crowds when I was human, and I found I liked them even less as a vampire. The noise and sweat and heat and fear-laced lust. It assaulted my senses. And the series of scathing whispers that snaked through the crowd grated on my nerves.

"Is that the new duchess?"

"She doesn't look like anything special to me."

"Isn't she the one who got Lydia in trouble?"

"Yeah, almost sucked her into a coma. What an amateur."

"I don't care. I'd let her bite me."

They were too close, and I'd had enough. I turned around and bared my fangs, hissing as they stumbled backward onto the dance floor.

"Sorry, ladies," I said, lisping since my fangs wouldn't allow my lips to fully close. "But it's time for us to make like bats and get the hell out of here."

Several pouted, but no one crept in on me. The girl in the

booth with Ursula parted the curtains, and Murphy ushered her onto the dance floor where her friends waited. She giggled as she showed them the puncture marks on the inside of her wrist. Not wanting to wait and see if it would motivate them to brave crossing me again, I ducked inside the booth.

Ursula had propped herself in one corner. Her legs were folded, the thigh-high slit of her emerald gown spread wide to reveal one long, pale leg. There were six empty juice glasses on the table. Apparently, she'd slipped in another snack after Lane had left to come and find me. Her liquid eyes were unfocused, and her chest rose and fell rapidly as if she'd just orgasmed. Maybe she had.

"I miss the eighties." She swallowed and tilted her head back against the booth wall. Her fangs were still out and tinted pink from her gorging. "Humans today are too concerned with their health. If I wanted vitamins and minerals in my blood, I would have stuck with the harem."

One of the arms waving above us slapped the inside of the booth. "I have some pain pills! I'll eat a handful," the girl attached to the arm said. I could only see a slice of her face over the wall, bleached bangs over too-wide, bloodshot eyes.

"Don't," I shouted back. "We're done for the night."

"Awwww," the girl and Ursula whined in unison.

"Time to go, Your Highness."

Ursula folded her arms like a spoiled teenager. "I'm the

princess. You don't tell me when it's time to go."

"I have a lead, and you're on the verge of starting a riot," I said, bracing a hand against one of the booth walls. There were enough people on the opposite side that I feared it would cave in on us at any moment. "If we don't leave now, Murphy will have to call the duke to request more guards to come and rescue us from the dogpile we're about to be on the bottom of."

"*Ugh*. Fine." Ursula stood suddenly and exited the booth in a blur. She was marinating in more power than she knew what to do with. It was reckless, and I hoped that it wore off before her path crossed with our council guests again.

I scrambled to stay on her heels as Murphy and Lane navigated the throng, carving a path toward the door. The club patrons crushed in around us, some reaching for Ursula until I stared them into retreat.

I searched for the bouncer at the front of the house, hoping he'd lend a hand. He didn't look prepared to, but then he pressed a finger to his earpiece and rolled his eyes. A second later, his face flushed a bright red. He'd probably forgotten that Radu could see everything from his security nest on the top floor.

When we finally reached the door, the bouncer put himself between the crowd and us, holding his arms out to cut them off. We hurried outside, and I pulled the door closed behind us.

Groupies were waiting in the parking lot, but less of them. Murphy's fangs extended, and the crowd promptly went back to minding their own business. Ursula eyed them greedily.

"This lead of yours better be a good one," she snapped. Her heels clicked on the pavement, and she folded her arms as we shepherded her along.

After feeding so intensely, her insides had to be on fire. The contrast in temperature was likely to blame for the goosebumps covering her pale flesh. I felt the bite of the wind, too, but my leather pants and long-sleeved blouse offered more protection.

"Eureka." Murphy patted a hand on the hood of our car and quickly opened the back door for Ursula and me to climb inside, safe from the prying eyes that lingered in the parking lot. Then he and Lane loaded into the front seat. "Let's get out of here before that doorman opens the floodgates."

Ursula gave me an annoyed glare. "Well? Tell Mr. Murphy where we're going," she demanded.

"Uh… Shouldn't we take you home first?" I asked. "If this *is* a good lead, we might be dealing with someone who has experience making bombs."

"Sounds like you should both be taken home," Murphy grumbled as he pulled the car out of the parking lot, not waiting for direction from me.

A swarm of clubgoers flailed their arms from the front of Bleeders. Ursula pressed the button to lower her window and waved back, flashing a toothy smile—sans fangs. She was handling the blood rush far better than I was sure I would have. Or so I thought.

"No one's going home," she said as Murphy rounded a corner, and the club and adoring donors disappeared.

Ursula's eyes were still dilated when she looked back at me. She rested her arm on the sill of her open window. The cold night air whipped inside the car, making her curls writhe around her face in a Medusa-esque halo.

"The last time I was surrounded by strangers who knew who I was, most of them were only interested in watching me suffer," she said with a soft, mirthless laugh. Then she licked a bit of dried blood from the corner of her mouth and grinned. "But now, I'm the princess. I take orders from the queen alone. The council can ask their questions and pass their judgements, but I'll decide when my night is over. Give Murphy the address, Jenna."

I swallowed but did as she bid. Murphy didn't try to argue either. He entered the address into the car's GPS, but the look he shot Lane held a silent command. The other guard shifted subtly in his seat. It didn't take X-ray vision to guess that he was retrieving his phone to text Dante a status update. Ursula wasn't fooled either.

"If the duke instructs you to drive us back to the manor, and you attempt to comply, I will exit this vehicle by any means necessary," Ursula said, making eye contact with Murphy as he glanced at her in the rearview mirror.

I didn't doubt her ability. With six fresh units of blood in her belly, I was betting she could pry an alligator's jaws open and rip it in half if she wanted to.

I just hoped it was enough to keep her in one piece if my lead ended in fireworks.

Chapter Sixteen

Tracy Young lived in Old North St. Louis. On the short drive over from Bleeders, I borrowed Murphy's phone and called Mandy to have her run a background check. Other than a 2010 drug charge for possession of meth when she lived in Denver, the woman was clean. And sober, too, I guessed.

Her sentence had included a month of rehab, and she'd passed the two random drug tests Radu had sprung on her during her employment with him. They'd been in the binder along with her application.

I was ashamed by how discouraging I found her sobriety. A meth lab mishap would have been a tidy way to close this investigation. It required plenty of nasty, combustible ingredients, too.

Drug training at the bat cave had been curiously brief. To be fair, drugs weren't exactly a vampiric vice. Werewolf addiction, on the other hand, did pose a problem, though Blood Vice only cared if an addict threatened supernatural society in some significant way. Like if a wolf got tweaked out of its mind and went on a killing spree. Otherwise, drug problems were left for the pack alphas to address.

Blood Vice was less *serve and protect* and more *conceal and deflect,* unfortunately. It had been the closest occupation to my human skillset, but I'd bombed it just as badly by caving to the blood bond I shared with Roman. It hadn't stopped the duke from coming to my rescue—not that it had felt like salvation at the time—and now I was somewhere in the realm of *smile and nod* thanks to the royal title. But not tonight.

Tonight, I was doing something worthwhile with my time. I probably would have been more excited about that if the job didn't include babysitting the princess. Or the council's looming ultimatum.

"According to DMV records, Young drives a gray '92 Mitsubishi Pajero—wait," Mandy said, pausing to snort. "No, that's right. *Pajero.* Wouldn't wanna be caught with your pants down in one of those." She cackled at some joke I didn't get.

"Pajero…" I pressed the phone in closer to my ear to hear over the sound of the wind coming through Ursula's open window. "I think those earlier models were kinda boxy like the Jeep Cherokees. I'll have to look up a picture of one to be sure."

"Already did," Mandy said. "Sending it now, along with Young's plate number." The phone chimed Murphy's cuckoo clock notification in my ear, announcing a new text message.

"Got it."

"You know," Mandy said thoughtfully, "I think I remember seeing something like that in the security video from the parking garage." That was promising. "You could be onto something, Jenna. Damn it! I should be there with you."

She huffed a frustrated sigh.

"I know," I said. "Maybe next time."

"If there is a next time."

We hung up as Murphy exited the Mark Twain Expressway, and I glanced down at the image of the vehicle and Young's plate number. I also took note of the time. Two in the morning. Five hours till sunrise. I wondered how long Dante would wait before sending the cavalry after us. Then my attention went back to the details Mandy had just shared.

Boxy gray SUV. Why did that sound familiar? Before I could think more about it, Murphy pulled up to a curb and cleared his throat.

"We're here," he said. "Do you see your mark's ride?"

I pushed the button to lower my window and scanned the cars and trucks along the curb and in the parking lot across the street. "It's hard to tell from here," I said, reaching for my door handle, but Murphy engaged the safety locks.

"I'll loop around the block a couple times," he said, eyeing me in the rearview mirror. "No sense in you getting out in the cold if you don't have to."

"Right." I decided not to point out the open windows and went back to my search.

This neighborhood wasn't the worst place to settle in St. Louis on a housekeeper's budget. There were a few odd buildings that were boarded up and surrounded by weed-choked sidewalks. A bit of litter in the gutters. An abandoned shopping cart, likely stolen from the grocery store we'd passed on the way in. But there were also one or two structures with historic charm and a large, modern apartment complex that looked as if it had been built within the last ten years or so.

Young lived in a duplex catty-corner from the apartments. The matching red front doors looked new, though the concrete stoop was crumbling and uneven. It seemed a common theme for the neighborhood, as if someone had come in with good intentions and then ran out of steam, money, or give-a-damn halfway through the facelift.

"Anything?" Murphy called from the front seat as we rolled past the parking lot a second time and came to a stop on the corner. The windows of Young's building were dark, and none of the nearby vehicles matched the description of hers.

"No." I slumped in my seat. "Damn it."

"We should call Nicks and have him put an agent or two on her place," Lane suggested.

"If this is a dead end, he'll accuse me of wasting resources and manpower," I said. "And if it isn't a dead end, he sure as shit won't give me credit for it."

"Is it true he fired you?" Murphy asked, eyeing me in the rearview mirror.

I snorted and folded my arms, which was answer enough.

If Murphy knew, that meant Nicks had filed paperwork of some sort to make it official. I wondered if I had any power as a duchess to prevent it—or better yet, any authority to fire *him*. The jerk.

Ursula grinned as if she approved of my predicament, but then her gaze slipped past me and out the window. "Would that be the gray SUV in question?"

I turned to watch as Young parked in front of her building and hopped out of the Mitsubishi. She was a curvy woman, which surprised me for a werewolf. Shifting burned a lot of calories. It was the reason Mandy could eat an entire pizza by herself, followed by half a tub of ice cream, and still look like a twig. Though, to be fair, she'd packed on some lean muscle since joining Blood Vice.

Unless Young had a second job as a professional butter taster, I was guessing she only shifted during the full moon— an unfortunate reality for a lot of low-income, city wolves. But better butter than bombs.

From the looks of Young, I could definitely believe she was moonlighting one way or another. Her jeans and sweatshirt were streaked with dirt. Bags hung under her eyes. Her ponytail was off center, and even in the dim streetlight, I could see how thin the soles of her shoes were as she climbed the steps to her front door.

Before I had a chance to warn Murphy, he put the car in

drive and turned the corner. Our headlights flashed across Young and her building, and she stopped digging through her purse to look up at us. One glance was all it took.

The luxury town car was out of place here. And creeping around during the witching hour made us extra suspect.

If I had any doubts that Young was involved with the opera house bombing, they *poofed* out of existence the moment she dropped her keys and shot off like a firework. She ducked between her duplex and the neighboring building. By the time Murphy stopped our car in front of the opening, she was almost to the garage sandwiched at the back of the narrow drive.

I tugged on my door handle, but the safety locks were still activated. "Sonofabitch!"

"We should call—" Murphy began. I didn't wait for him to finish. I pushed my back against the door and angled myself up and out through the open window, bracing one hand on the roof of the car until my legs were free, too. When I turned around, I nearly collided with Ursula.

"How the—?"

"I'm coming with you," she said, anxious energy animating her voice.

"Like hell, you are."

"Skye, Your Highness," Murphy pleaded as he and Lane joined us. "Get back in the car."

Ursula's fangs extended as Lane reached for her arm, and he froze, unwilling to risk her wrath after all the blood she'd had tonight.

I sidestepped around the princess and tore after Young. The woman had reached the closed garage door. She bent down to test the lock, but the door didn't budge. The buildings were crammed together, and I could see no other escape. I had her cornered, though the sense of victory stalled when she turned and raced back toward me.

I slapped my hip, instinctively reaching for a firearm that wasn't there, and felt the thick case of my stun gun through my front pocket instead. Before I could withdraw it, Young spun around again.

I stopped in the middle of the drive, waiting to see what she would do. If she tried to rush me, I wanted a buffer so I'd see it coming.

She darted toward the corner made by the garage and duplex and then leapt, one sneaker pushing off the garage before the other found purchase on the mismatched brick of the duplex. The third step up was less graceful. Her foot lost traction before her chest had fully cleared the roof of the garage.

Young grunted as the gutter caught her across the breasts, but she hooked an elbow over the edge in time to keep from falling. Her sneakers scuffed against the cinder-block face of the garage, and the gutter creaked, but she managed to pull herself up and rolled onto the roof and out of sight just as Ursula and Murphy reached me.

"Don't see that every day." Murphy clamped a hand on my shoulder. His breath was labored, but I was sure it had more to do with nerves than the sprint down the driveway. "Lane's calling Nicks," he added as I shrugged off his hand and took off toward the street.

"Super," I shouted back at him. "We can borrow his cuffs after I take down Young."

"Come on, Skye!" Murphy swore and gave chase, but Ursula was already a step ahead of him. I paused at the opening to the street, trying to decide which way to loop around, and the princess all but tripped over me.

"You go that way," she ordered, pointing east, then took off in the opposite direction. Her sequined dress glittered in the streetlights. I was impressed by how little the stilettos seemed to slow her down. Murphy breezed past me and hurried after her, looking like a groveling prom date in his gold suit.

"Get back in the car," he shouted, thrusting a finger toward the empty backseat. Lane stood behind the open door, a cell phone pressed to his ear. He waved a hand, urging me to follow Murphy's instruction.

I ignored them both and listened to my sire for a change.

My boots made less noise than Ursula's heels, but I knew that wouldn't be of much use. A wolf could hear and smell trouble a mile away even in their human form, though they were at their strongest when furry and four-legged.

If Young shifted on top of the garage roof, I would have a harder time subduing her. But if she decided to climb down the opposite side in human form, there was a good chance I could get to her before things got too weird for any busybodies peeking through their curtains.

The cold air ached in my lungs, growing more uncomfortable with each inhale as I raced down the sidewalk. The buildings were practically on top of one another, with tall gates cutting off in-between access. I checked one and found it locked. *Fuck my luck.*

I rounded the corner, and my mood flipped like a coin. A narrow alley dissected the block, running between the two tight rows of buildings. The gap was wide enough that I didn't think Young could leap the distance—in either form.

I counted the backsides of the buildings as I ran past them, trying to remember how many had flanked Young's to the east. Three? Maybe four. It was darker down the alley, with only a few halos of light spilling over rickety privacy fences and crumbling block walls. But then a garage door that matched the one she'd scaled caught my attention, and I paused to squint at the roofline.

"Your Highness!" Murphy's desperate voice echoed down the alley. I was sure the growl that followed meant he'd spotted me, too. Between him and the sharp clack of the princess's footwear, we wouldn't surprise Young in the slightest.

"We meet again," Ursula said, stopping beside me.

My gaze dropped from the garage roof, and I glanced at the line of mismatched fences and retaining walls on the opposite side of the alley. Could Young have had enough time to leap over one? If we hadn't caught her exiting the lane, that meant she was hiding somewhere around here. If only Mandy had come with us.

"Nicks is sure to have a wolf agent with him," Murphy said, picking up on my frustration. "We should go back to the car, let the professionals handle this."

"Professionals?" I snapped. "Just because I was fired doesn't make me any less of a professional, and I think you're forgetting that the council *asked* me to handle this. It's part of the evaluation."

"They asked you to solve the case," he shouted back at me. "Not to single-handedly take down everyone involved."

"Single-handedly?" It was Ursula's turn to take offense. She sniffed and glared at Murphy. "A young scion should always be able to depend on her sire."

"You can save that BS for the stuffed shirts." The guards

rarely broke protocol where the royal family was concerned, but Murphy was the occasional exception to the rule. He sighed and rubbed a hand over his sweaty face. "If either of you go and get yourselves killed, that evaluation won't mean shit," he said. "Did you even once stop and think that might be the council's aim here?"

I'd considered it, but my ambition had outweighed the fear by a long shot. What surprised me was that Ursula seemed to feel the same way. She sighed and reached for Murphy's shoulder, but before her hand made contact, a streak of gray fur dropped out of the sky and torpedoed into Murphy's chest, knocking him off his feet. His back hit a paint-chipped privacy fence and uprooted a loose post. He managed to throw up his arm as the gray wolf snapped in his face and then screamed when teeth clamped over his wrist.

Young had done what any reasonable wolf hoping to thwart an ambush would have. She'd taken down the largest of her opponents first, making the best use of the element of surprise. She probably thought two petite lady vamps dressed for a night on the town wouldn't put up much of a fight. Boy, was she wrong.

Ursula snatched the wolf by the tail and dragged her away from Murphy. Young was fearsome as a beastie, her dark fur standing on end and ears laid flat against her head. When she released Murphy to twist and snap at Ursula, the princess gave her tail a mean jerk. The motion lifted the wolf off the ground and flung her into the closed garage door behind us.

Young shook her muzzle as she scrambled to her feet, but by then I was ready for her. I pressed the business end of the stun gun to the side of her shoulder. A crackle of electricity, followed by a sharp whine, and it was lights out, wolf girl.

A regular stun gun wouldn't have done much more than annoy a werewolf, but the silver prongs were a supernatural bonus feature. According to the box it had come in, it worked like a charm on vamps, too. I hadn't tested that claim yet, but it did make me feel better about having to leave my guns behind so much of the time.

Ursula smirked as Young's unconscious body writhed on the pavement, breaking and healing itself as she slowly shifted into her human form. "Not so big and bad now, are we?"

Chapter Seventeen

The last time I'd been in Blood Vice's St. Louis field office, Vanessa Sorano had invoked the right to a blood duel. The former captain had not been thrilled when she discovered that I'd been snacking on her pledged scion. Like a coward, I'd tucked tail and fled for my life. From the sneers shot my way as we entered the building now, I guessed no one had forgotten.

I would have felt more confident coming back here if I could have marched Young through the front doors myself. Nicks had arrived minutes after our alley scuffle to cuff her and load her into the back of his SUV.

The stun gun hadn't knocked Young out for very long, but since her clothes were on the roof of the garage, Murphy had loaned her his shiny gold jacket. It was hard to feel like a fearless hero when the defeated villain was a shivering, naked woman. But covering her up was all we'd gotten to do before Blood Vice showed.

"Your Highness." An agent I hadn't met before bowed as he caught sight of the princess. "What can I do for you?"

"I've got them," Nicks said, appearing in the mouth of the hall that split off from the main floor. He'd been expecting us, but the look on his face made me think that he'd hoped we wouldn't show—that we'd get a flat tire or be run off the road by a semi. He carried a manila folder under one arm and a chip on his shoulder. "Follow me—Your Highness, Your Grace," he added when Murphy shot him a dark look.

I was more than happy to escape the mocking stares of my former colleagues. I missed the work. The people I'd worked with? Not so much. To them, I was just a random green fang who had been rewarded for screwing the pooch. They weren't wrong.

Nicks led us to the back of the building where the interrogation rooms were located, and we all squeezed inside the first one we passed. I was shocked to find Dante and Beauclair waiting in the dark room, along with another Blood Vice agent.

Through the wide viewing window that spanned one wall, I could see Young sitting at a table. She still wore Murphy's satin jacket, but her hands were uncuffed now, and she furiously worried the ends of the jacket's too-long sleeves. Her nails were chewed to the quick, and she looked as though she'd been crying.

Captain Nicks closed the observation room door and scowled at us—at all seven of us, counting the other agent I didn't recognize. "It's not really necessary for any of you to be here. You don't *all* intend to stay, do you?" he said. "Could take me a long while to crack her. If there's anything to be cracked, that is." He shot me a skeptical frown.

"Is this not the suspect that the duchess—Agent Skye—discovered?" Beauclair asked. She perched on a stool near a computer desk in the far corner of the room, her legs crossed and folded hands resting over the cap of one knee.

"The *duchess* did discover this woman," Nicks admitted through clenched teeth. "Though her involvement in the case is still unknown."

"Then why is the duchess not handling the interrogation?" Beauclair prodded, a frown pinching her arrogant face.

"That's not how we do things here—" Nicks scoffed, and his face flushed with annoyance as he shifted his weight from one foot to the other. "Interrogation is for seasoned agents—not former agents who should have better things to do with their royal spare time. This is serious work we do here."

My jaw tightened, but Dante's hand touched my shoulder before I could lash out at the captain.

"What we do with our *royal spare time* is none of your concern," Dante said to Nicks. "However, our work is every bit as serious as yours, and you would do well to remember that."

Nicks would also do well to remember that the duke had hired him in the first place, but Dante didn't say that. He didn't have to.

"Of course, Your Grace." Nicks cleared his throat.

"Though I must insist on sitting in for this session. Ms. Skye is no longer a registered agent with Blood Vice. You approved the paperwork yourself—"

"Did you happen to *read* the paperwork, Fredrick?" Dante snapped.

"Well, I-I've been busy with the investigation—" Nicks' giant brow creased as he struggled to come up with a better answer.

"Because if you did," Dante went on, "you would know that I amended your request and that the only reason Jenna Skye is no longer a registered agent with Blood Vice is because she is now registered as Jenna Lilosa—Agent Lilosa."

Agent Lilosa. I liked the sound of that. I resisted the urge to kiss Dante's face off.

"I see," Nicks said. To his credit, he didn't offer further comment on the duke's decision.

"I don't mind if you sit in," I said, sucking in the corners of my mouth to keep my grin from growing too smug. "Since you didn't share the entire case file before—with the employee and guest interviews—I have to assume the lab has produced test results that I'm unfamiliar with, too. I'll need someone nearby to refute or confirm anything I get out of Young."

Nicks grimaced at the idea of playing my fact-checker sidekick, but then his gaze shifted back to Dante. "Let's get this over with."

"That's the spirit," I said, swinging my fist with sarcastic cheer.

I didn't feel especially official in my cropped lace blouse, but at least my all-black outfit matched the captain's uniform. I'd been the most modest of my party at Bleeders, despite Ursula's streetwalker comment, though the once-over Nicks gave me as we stepped out into the hallway suggested he thought even less of my attire.

"Just let me do the talking," he said. "You might still be an agent on the books, but I'm the captain here, understand?"

"You're the captain," I parroted back at him.

He nodded and smoothed a hand over his buzz cut before opening the interrogation room door and waving me inside. Then he pulled out my chair for me. He had to look like a gentleman for our eager audience.

I smiled politely and sat down, folding my hands over the table at the same time Young removed hers, dropping them into her lap.

"I haven't done nothin' wrong," she blurted. "I want a lawyer."

"If you *haven't done nothin' wrong*, what need do you have for a lawyer?" I asked.

Nicks cleared his throat and shot me a wide-eyed glare that I ignored. He could be captain all he wanted, but as he'd pointed out numerous times, I was the duchess. And, like my sire, there were only so many people I was willing to tolerate bossing me around. Nicks was not one of them.

"Are you Tracy Young, former member of the Washburn Pack in Denver?" Nicks asked, flipping open the file he'd brought with him.

The woman's bottom lip trembled, but she nodded in reply. "They kicked me out years ago, though. I moved to Missouri for a fresh start."

"And you work for Radu Vlad as part of the housekeeping staff at the Nightfall Opera House?"

"Well, I *used* to," Young said. "Mr. Vlad called and told me what happened—"

"You were spotted leaving the parking garage near the opera house shortly after the explosion last night," I said, jumping right to it. It wasn't a full-on bluff, considering Mandy had remembered a vehicle similar to the gray Mitsubishi.

"Look, I was just in the wrong place at the wrong time," Young tried again. She pressed her fingers over her eyes and sucked in a shaky breath. "I was scared. I was going to come in and give a statement. Really, I was," she stammered.

Nicks was too surprised to reprimand me this time. I decided to charge ahead before he found his bearings. If he took control of the questioning again, we'd be here till sunrise, confirming every boring detail about Young's life that we all already knew.

"If you wanted us to have your statement so badly, why run?"

"I didn't know who you were," she sobbed. "I thought… I don't know what I thought."

"You must have had some horrific idea in your head to tear off the way you did," I said. "Who did you think was coming after you?" When she didn't answer right away, I resorted to the half-bluffs again. "We found a partially-burnt letter containing your handwriting near the origin of the blast. Our experts are restoring and deciphering it as we speak."

I thought Nicks was going to shit a pineapple, but his irate attention was quickly dispersed as Young stumbled over her answer.

"What? No—that's—it's…a personal letter, okay? Nothin' about bombs or anything like that."

"Who was he, Tracy?" I pressed.

Her eyes watered, and she swallowed hard. She was afraid to answer the question as if it might somehow come back to bite her, but I could offer no guarantees. If she were in any way responsible for the bombing, Beauclair would see to it that Young paid the price.

"It's obvious you cared for this man," Nicks said, joining the conversation now that it had stalled. "His family deserves to know what happened to him."

"I was his only family," Young said, sniffling. "His name was Bart Haulette."

"Do you know why he bombed the opera house?"

"He didn't mean to." Young's brows drew together, and she ran both hands under her eyes, wiping away the tears that spilled down her cheeks. "This is all my fault—*no*, this is all Arnie's fault."

"Arnie? Arnie Moreau?" I leaned forward, and Nicks did the same, clutching the case file with both hands.

"Yeah." Young scoffed. "He's a real piece of work. I thought that's who sent you when you showed up at my place. He threatened to kill me if I went to the cops. Now that I'm here, I'm as good as dead. Might as well make a little hell for that bastard while I can."

"We can protect you from the Moreau Pack," Nicks offered. I noticed how he hadn't insisted that we'd protect her from everyone who might wish her harm. If Beauclair marched in here and demanded that Young face trial for whatever part she'd played in the bombing, there wasn't a damned thing anyone could do about it.

"No, you can't," Young said, resignation tightening the lines of her face. "I met Bart in Denver. He was a...*chemist*."

"He's the reason for the meth charge on your record?" I asked.

Young nodded. "It's what got me kicked out of the pack."

"Then why stay with him?" Nicks asked. I nudged his knee with mine, willing him to zip it. Going all Judgy McJudgerson would only make her clam up again.

"I accidentally scratched Bart," she confessed. "I turned him, and if the pack had found out, they would have executed me. Bart loved me—in his own stupid way. He promised to quit cooking and dealing, and I promised to help him learn to be a wolf. We moved out here to start over together. We'd only been in St. Louis for a few months when I bumped into an old packmate of mine. She told us about a werewolf-run, Cajun restaurant in Dutchtown."

"Snake Eyes." I'd been to the hole-in-the-wall joint before. It belonged to Arnie. It was more bar than restaurant, but the beta of the Moreau Pack made most of his money from the illegal gambling he did out of the back room—the place where I'd taken a bite out of him the last time our paths had crossed.

Young's eyes darkened as though she'd acquired a far less satisfying memory from the place. "Bart was a charismatic guy. He caught Arnie's attention right off, and soon enough, he was working for the pack. It was just small errands, at first. Sometimes, Arnie would ask him to work security on busy nights. But then, the pack alpha, Marcel, got involved. Bart started making trips out of state for conferences and to pick up bulk supplies. He said the restaurant was expanding, that they were going to start offering catering."

"Did you suspect he was lying to you?" Nicks asked. Young shook her head in earnest.

"He had all these brochures and cookbooks and such— really sold me on the idea. That's why I let him take my car so much and rode the bus to work. I was so stupid." She covered her face with her hands and took a few deep breaths before going on.

"When I was gettin' ready to go in Saturday morning, I couldn't find my keycard for the opera house. So, I took an earlier bus, thinking I'd left it behind in one of the rooms or the cleaning closet. I wanted to have plenty of time to find it before my shift started. What I found instead was Bart, carrying boxes in through the side entrance.

"I followed him upstairs, to the top floor suites where he'd set up in one of the vacant rooms. I thought he was cooking meth again, and I was *so* mad. He tried to tell me he was making history, that he was fighting for our freedom so we could live as werewolves were intended to, without bloodsucking overlords—no offense," she said, wincing nervously. I shrugged and nodded for her to continue, disregarding the way Nicks' shoulders had squared beside me.

"I broke up with Bart before giving him a chance to explain himself any better than that," Young said. "But when

I took my keycard and car keys back, he got irrational and violent. He slapped me, and I panicked. Shoved him right into the slow cookers he was using to mix his concoctions. I stormed out and made it all the way down to the main floor on the elevator when the explosion happened."

She swallowed and looked down at her fingers peeking out from the ends of the gold jacket. It seemed so big on her, like a child playing dress up.

"You *thought* he was cooking meth?" I asked, sure there was more to be learned—something especially damning that would prove Arnie's involvement. "Did you confront Arnie about it? Is that why he threated to kill you if you went to the authorities?"

Young sighed. She looked as if she hadn't slept in days, and it was finally catching up with her. "I found a bunch of scrap silver in the back of my car, stuffed down in catering boxes. That's when I knew something else was going on. I went to Snake Eyes and dumped the silver in the parking lot. I was too afraid to go inside. I stayed the night with a friend, not sure if my own apartment was even safe.

"Arnie called the next morning from a blocked number. He said he knew I'd returned the silver. He actually thanked me before threatening to cut my throat in my sleep if I mentioned his name to anyone. And he told me to burn anything of Bart's with the logo for Hearty Harem on it."

"Hearty Harem?" My blood vision drenched the room as I shot up from my chair. My head snapped around, and I stared through the one-way glass, finding Dante outlined in red. The panic in his expression mirrored my fear.

Dawn was fast approaching, but our night was far from over.

Chapter Eighteen

Dante stood near the window in Nicks' office, one finger nudging aside the blinds so he could see the parking lot. His other hand gripped his cell phone until his knuckles turned white. It was the sort of paranoid anxiety I expected from Ursula rather than the duke, and it tightened the knot that had formed in my stomach the second Young had mentioned Hearty Harem.

"Agent Starsgard has confirmed that the equipment currently in the harem kitchen—left behind by Haulette's staff—is tamper-free," Dante said in a hushed voice. "The next meal delivery is scheduled for sunrise. I told Belinda not to cancel it or to alarm our household with this discovery as Nicks suggested. There could be a mole in the harem. We cannot afford to tip them off."

Beauclair sat in one of the guest chairs in front of Nicks' desk, her arms folded, fingers nervously drumming the sleeves of her lavender power suit. Ursula sat in the chair opposite her, looking every bit the councilwoman's evil counterpart with her glitzy gown and flaming locks. The rest of us— Murphy, Lane, and I—huddled in the corner near the office door, eagerly awaiting the captain's return.

"I don't agree with keeping this from the other council members," Beauclair said, clearly irked that she not only ranked lower than the duke but Nicks, too, in this situation. Her take-charge personality didn't mesh well with sitting and waiting. The suspense wasn't doing much good for me either.

The office door opened, and Nicks appeared in the threshold.

"Public records show that Haulette purchased a warehouse in Dutchtown not half a mile from Snake Eyes," the captain said, adjusting the straps of his ballistic vest. "I have a raid team ready to go."

"Do you have an extra vest?" I asked. Dante drew in a deep breath, but he didn't try to talk me down. He let Nicks attempt to instead.

"Your Grace…" The captain's brow pinched with genuine fear. "I would not be doing my job if I put any of the royal family in harm's way."

I didn't imagine he'd be *keeping* his job if I ended up dead on his watch either. However self-serving the incentive might've been, I was glad for it. Dying once had been enough.

"The duchess is also a trained agent," Beauclair pointed out. "And the council demands proof of her *talents* as such in order to assess whether the princess is being reckless or noble with her probationary scion."

The veil of Beauclair's support was beginning to wear thin for me, especially after Murphy had voiced his concerns in the alley behind Young's duplex.

"Then I shall require a vest, as well," Dante said, crossing the room to place his hand on my shoulder. He gave me a tender, apologetic frown, but there was nothing to forgive. Learning that he'd vetoed Nicks' request to can me had said it all.

Ursula's dead stare directed at Beauclair was unreadable. Did she regret the cover story she'd baked up on the spot when the council questioned us about Wikes? Would she confess now to keep me out of danger? Or would she snap and rip Beauclair's throat out where the hateful woman sat just a few feet away? I couldn't even decide which of those options would be worse.

"I'll take one of those vests, too," Ursula finally said, surprising everyone. "And I suppose you'll also need one, my lady—if you're to collect adequate *proof* for your evaluation."

"I have several out in the car," Murphy offered as Nicks sputtered in protest.

"This is insanity!" His voice rose sharply, and he moved to fill more of the doorway, blocking our exit. "We have less than two hours until sunrise."

"Then I guess we better get a move on," Murphy said, slapping Nicks on the shoulder hard enough to move him aside. The captain sized up the duke's head of security, but the only thing Nicks had over Murphy was an extra inch of forehead. If they came to blows, my money was on my sparring partner.

Nicks' lips pressed into a flat line as he made the right call and backed down. The rest of us filed out after Murphy—even Beauclair, though she hadn't seemed especially happy about being caught in her own snare. But how could she show her face to the council if she sent half the royal family into a potential bomb zone while she cowered halfway across town?

I guessed being a professional cutthroat was risky business.

The new coat I'd gotten for Midwinter held my pair of .40 caliber Reaper TDs in the deep breast pockets stitched into the lining. I'd left it in the car at Bleeders, not wanting to be dogpiled by security, but I had missed its luxury and warmth—and the weight of the firearms—in the biting cold.

With a ballistic vest, the coat didn't allow for much range of motion. I didn't like the idea of spoiling the pricey garment with bullet holes either. Dante would no doubt buy me a hundred more, but a few decades of middle-class human frugality were not so easily discarded.

I dug my pistols out of the coat pockets and hooked the clips of their holsters onto my vest under each arm. It wasn't the way I would have preferred to pack them, but after shortening the straps of Murphy's spare shoulder holster as far as they'd go, it was still too big. This would have to do.

Dante watched me with a deepening frown. "I ought to have a firearm," he said, though it sounded more like a question. "You should not be doing this alone."

"I won't be alone. There are at least two dozen agents in Nicks' raid team," I said, taking in the scramble of men as they suited up and loaded into SUVs outside the field office. "If Beauclair has a problem with that, then I think we'd be within rights to accuse her of conspiring to indirectly murder a member of House Lilith—which would mean I could challenge her to a blood duel. Wouldn't that be fun?"

Dante frowned at the idea, missing my sarcasm entirely. "I meant that you should not be doing this alone without *me*," he clarified. "As my beloved, I feel compelled to defend you, however I am able."

"When's the last time you were in a shoot-out?" I asked, my eyes trailing across the dark parking lot to where Nicks grumbled as he helped Beauclair into a vest.

"1865."

Dante's answer caught me off guard. I supposed it made sense, though. That was when the Civil War had ended, and also the year Alexander had turned him. Dante had risen as the Duke of House Lilith, a royal scion to be sheltered and defended. He was physically stronger than I was, to be sure.

Vampiric maturity had its benefits. But in modern combat, he was more liability than asset.

"Sounds like you might be a little rusty," I said, readjusting the straps of my vest. Dante placed a hand on mine, drawing my gaze back to him.

"I am afraid for you, Jenna, but I do not know how to help. All I know is that I would give my life for yours."

"I know." I took his hand and pressed it over my heart. "I would give my life for yours, too. But it's less likely to come to that if you stay clear of the fight."

Dante was used to having all the answers and being the calm, collected authority of our household—of our family. There was a traditional chivalry about him that I occasionally loathed but often admired. He wanted to protect Ursula, Audrey, and me from all the dangers of the world outside the comfort of the manor.

It wasn't so much a matter of him thinking us incapable— or at least, he didn't find *me* incapable. If that had been the case, he wouldn't have approved my request to train at the bat cave. Coddling was just his vintage love language. For royal scions with enemies at every turn, a little sheltering wasn't always such a bad thing.

But what good was eternal life if you were too afraid to live it?

The frightening possibility that Arnie was preparing to deliver a bomb to the manor put the fear of Lilith in every able body Nicks had recruited for the attack—or counterattack, as it were. Young had unintentionally taken out Haulette before he'd put the finishing touches on his Free Blooder lunch bomb, but the boxes of scrap silver suggested that he'd had far deadlier intentions.

Establishing a legit company under a patsy's name in order to launch an attack on the royal family seemed a little too ambitious for Arnie Moreau. I guessed that most of the braining involved with that venture had been done by Arnie's brother, Marcel.

I'd never met the Moreau Pack alpha, but I'd despised him for some time now. There were plenty of horror stories to be had, but Mandy's gutted me the worst. She knew Marcel. *Intimately.* She hadn't spelled it out, but I was sure he'd been the one to turn her at the Scarlett Inn. And that had only been the beginning of his reign of terror over her.

No one had spotted Marcel in St. Louis since the shifty brothel had shut down, but I had no doubt that he was still at the helm of the Moreau Pack, even if he let Arnie parade around as the front man most of the time. The alpha was more elusive than Bigfoot, and I doubted we'd find him among the worker bees tonight. The premature explosion at the opera house was sure to have spooked him back under the rock he'd been hiding under.

Ursula and Lane joined Dante and Beauclair in the car the duke and councilwoman had taken to Blood Vice, while I rode shotgun with Murphy. I needed to stay focused, and I couldn't do that with Dante's fearful, longing gaze cutting me to the core. Besides, they'd been instructed to keep well clear of the scene once we arrived.

Murphy followed Nicks' taillights across the city to Dutchtown, creeping in on the opposite side of the neighborhood from Snake Eyes. If we didn't find Arnie and whoever else he had on his brother's terrorist payroll at Haulette's warehouse, the restaurant was our next stop.

"I don't care what the council lady has to say about it—I'm going in with you," Murphy said, his eyes leaving the road for a split second to stare at me. I figured that had been his plan when he changed out of Ursula's shiny club ensemble and into the all-purpose backup suit he'd dug out of the trunk of the car along with the vests.

He'd also produced the cape of his guard uniform and insisted that I wear it. The thick, velvety material was warm. But more useful than that, it was made out of the same fiber that a lot of bomb blankets were crafted from. My only reservation about it was the bright red color. I looked like a comic book superhero—or an eye-catching target for a charging bull or *werewolf.*

"I wouldn't mind having someone I trust watching my back," I said. "That might even keep the duke from having a nervous breakdown."

"Yeah, I think he might like you." Murphy's humor should have eased the tension, but it only made me wonder about the stupid things people did in the name of love—even with centuries of wisdom under their belt.

"I'm not a very safe girl to like," I said, frowning out my window at the blur of dark scenery as we flew down Route 30.

A half-full moon hung high above. Its pale light caught on the patches of snow dotting the rooftops of the homes in the neighborhood that bordered the industrial park we'd turned into. The ride had been a short one, but not nearly long enough to quiet the bats fluttering around in my stomach.

Several warehouses crowded the block Haulette's was on. Nicks could have used them to hide the small fleet of SUVs if he'd wanted to, but we were so close now, any wolves inside knew they had company.

The building Haulette had purchased must've been a factory in another life. Only a handful of windows broke up the brick façade, scattered just under the roofline. They were each cracked an inch or two, just enough to ruin any chance of surprise.

Nicks whipped his SUV into the parking lot, blocking off two white vans with the Hearty Harem logo stamped on their sliding doors. Three more Blood Vice SUVs blocked the entrance to the factory, leaving Murphy to park on the curb across the street, in front of a row of storage units.

Half a block behind us on the same curb, Dante's car rolled to a stop. I wanted to activate the Eye of Blood so I could see him through the tinted windows, but I knew that would only make this harder. I couldn't afford distractions right now.

A third car—one I recognized from the manor garage— flew past Dante's and parked illegally on the curb in front of us. Mandy climbed out of the driver's seat at the same time I stepped out of Murphy's car. She carried her K9 vest under one arm and wore only an oversized tee shirt. No pants or shoes.

"W-what are you *doing?*" I stammered, wondering who was keeping an eye on Laura.

"My job," Mandy snapped. She shoved the K9 vest at me and then yanked off her shirt before dropping to all fours. Murphy swore and turned away as her bones cracked with the onset of her shift.

A soft whimper wheezed through her nose as it elongated into a muzzle. She'd gotten faster at the transformation, but it didn't look any less painful. Thick, dark fur erupted from her flesh, and her delicate wrists and ankles stretched as her fingers curled into claws.

When Mandy finished, the black coat of her wolf blended with the shadows, making her golden eyes glow in the dark. She scuffed a paw on the road at my feet, urging me to get on with it. I dropped the K9 vest over her back and knelt to fasten the buckles under her belly.

A thundering clamor drew our attention back to the factory. Several of Nicks' men wielded a battering ram. They took aim at the factory's steel door a second time, and the sound of metal on metal ripped through the night again.

Frantic voices filtered through the windows. Mandy's ears twitched. The fur along her spine lifted, and she bared her teeth.

"Arnie?" I guessed. She barked once in affirmation.

"We get him, the rest of the pack will scatter or yield," Murphy said, putting a finger in his good ear as the battering ram made contact a third time, and the steel door swung inward, thudding against an interior wall.

"And the council will get lost," I added. Mandy yipped and hopped anxiously on her front paws.

"Right. And the house won't go kaboom," Murphy said, nodding as if he'd understood her.

"I just hope we don't go kaboom first." I drew one of my

pistols and led the way, chasing after Nicks and the swarm of Blood Vice agents funneling inside the building.

Chapter Nineteen

In a just world, scumbags like Arnie Moreau would have a balanced ratio of brains to morals. Like Saturday morning cartoon villains. In the *real* world, that was just wishful thinking. And Arnie had just enough smarts to muddle an already complicated situation.

The second the factory had been breached, the lights went out. Wolves could see just fine in the dark. Of all the agents on hand, I'd only picked out two that I knew were wolves. Most of the daywalkers worked the sunup shift, leaving sundown for the vamp agents. Still, I was sure Nicks' men had the standard-issue, night vision goggles.

I had the Eye of Blood, and it didn't take much coaxing to activate it with all the silver zipping through the main floor of the building. A bullet snagged my ponytail, and I gasped as the massive room blinked into crimson existence.

Towering pallet racks divided the space, their shelves filled with commercial cookware and bulk cleaning supplies. A newer walk-in freezer filled the back corner of the room near another exit that Nicks and two more agents had secured. They stood with their backs to the barred steel door, returning fire at Arnie's men with their Moba M4s.

The Moreau Pack was armed with less sophisticated weapons—shotguns and switchblades—but they were fast. A wiry, shirtless man dove through an opening on a low shelf and delivered half a dozen kidney stabs to an agent before the vampire could even get off a single shot.

A few wolves soon joined the mix, and things got even messier.

"Skye," Murphy hissed behind me. "I can't see shit. Where are you?"

"I'm here." I touched his shoulder, causing him to jump. We hadn't reached the heart of the skirmish yet, but the pallet rack we took cover behind wouldn't keep us from the fight for long.

Mandy crept under a shelf to get a better view, searching for Arnie. He was the only one of these creeps who could turn tonight into a win for the home team. I wanted to hand-deliver him to Beauclair, collect my cookie, and call it a night.

When Mandy's soft growl broke through the din, I glanced around the room to see if I could spy our quarry. Even with the blood vision, there was so much happening, I didn't know where to look first.

Another bullet ripped past me, and I gasped as Murphy pulled me down behind a stack of portable food tables. He clutched a pistol that matched mine to his chest, too blind to know where to safely point it.

Mandy shot out from under the shelf before I spotted what had caught her attention. My gaze trailed ahead of her, trying to guess her path as she cut around the room.

In the corner opposite the walk-in was a concrete staircase. It was open to the main floor up to the first landing before it curled around and out of view. I'd looked up just in time to catch sight of the back of a leather jacket stamped with the faded insignia of the Moreau Pack.

Arnie.

Mandy followed him, taking the stairs ten at a time in her wolfy form. She was never good at waiting for orders—least of all from me.

I grabbed Murphy's hand and dragged him down the aisle created by the pallet racks, taking the long way around to reduce our chances of getting shot. Gunfire filled the room with flashes of light and a roaring chorus that made my ears ring.

When we reached the stairs, I pushed Murphy up ahead of me and climbed the steps with my back pressed to the far railing, pistol aimed behind us in case anyone became too interested in us.

Nicks' rifle tilted upward briefly, but then he realized who we were. The small *oh* his mouth formed was accentuated by the bug-eyed goggles affixed to his face, but he quickly resumed guarding the back door as a wolf charged him.

A dim security light lit the second stretch of stairs after the landing. The relief on Murphy's face was intense. Walking through a warzone blind was not for the faint of heart, and he'd done it for me—even if he'd been unable to do much more than play the part of a not-so-human shield. Vampire or not, bullets still hurt, and a strategically placed silver one could be deadly for anyone.

"I was useless down there." Murphy's brow was damp, and his eyes blinked fiercely as his pupils constricted in the spill of light.

"They're managing," I said. "You get a gold star for not shooting up a room you couldn't see that was half-full of our people."

He placed his free hand on the wall as we reached the top landing, catching his breath before ducking his head around the corner to take a quick assessment of our next step—or at least, *my* next step.

"Lights are out up here, too," Murphy said, jaw flexing.

A growl drew our attention to the landing below as a black wolf appeared from around the corner. It was running so fast, its hind end grazed the wall as it turned to head up the flight we stood at the top of.

Murphy aimed without hesitation and sank a single round between the creature's eyes, sending it on a rude detour over the railing, back to the factory floor below. A surprised yelp told us there'd soon be more where the first had come from.

"I'll hold the stairwell," Murphy said. "You find Mandy

and stop that prick from doing something stupid."

I gave him a two-fingered salute before taking off in the direction I hoped Mandy had gone.

The loft was suspended over a good third of the factory floor. A paint-chipped, metal railing created a wide balcony across one side, while the other end of the loft was boxed in with more pallet racks and long work tables that held chop saws and several stamped catering boxes full of mismatched, tarnished silverware.

Three windows stretched across the far wall, framing the moon as she dropped lower in the sky. Her light slipped through the glass and caught on everything the invading wind pushed around the room—fast food trash and metallic dust.

My heart raced as I searched for Mandy and Arnie. Beyond the balcony at my back, shots echoed up from below, and flickers of gunfire reached for the ceiling. It was still unbearably loud, but as I moved deeper into the loft, I was able to make out the harsh words being exchanged over a nearby work table tucked behind more shelves.

"Leave them where they are," Arnie hissed. "Just set the charges. We'll shift and slip out through the sewer access under the loading dock."

"But the plan—" the other man argued.

"Fuck the plan, Terry." Arnie growled, and something heavy smashed against a wall. I swallowed a gasp as my Blood

Vision surged, and the men appeared through the racks, their body heat glowing like auras around them.

"I haven't even got the silver in the pots yet," Terry protested.

"Doesn't matter. We already know the formula packs enough punch to bring this entire building down on top of those fanged fucks."

"But *our* guys are down there, too."

"We have more," Arnie said. "Collateral damage. If we don't do this now, we go down with the ship. Understand?"

The callousness of Arnie's voice made me wonder how anyone could be stupid enough to trust this asshat with their life. If he wasn't rolling on his partners to get out of a jam with Blood Vice, he was using them up like pawns on a chessboard.

Terry reminded me of a Nirvana poster I'd had as a kid. Flannel shirt. Long, messy hair. I almost admired his loyalty to the rest of the pack—unlawful as they were—but from the clear safety goggles and respirator mask dangling around his neck, it was obvious that he was just as guilty of the horrors Hearty Harem had planned.

From the sheer volume of supplies in the warehouse, I had no doubt that the opera house and the duke's manor were the only targets on their list. I prayed that the three vans out front were the only ones they owned and that we hadn't arrived too late to stop any from departing with an explosive delivery.

Arnie squeezed Terry's shoulder, pressing one thumbnail dangerously close to the other man's Adam's apple. The gesture caused his leather jacket to gape open, revealing a sawed-off shotgun strapped across his chest. It was a primal, universal threat. If Terry refused to follow orders, he wouldn't have to worry about Blood Vice. The alpha's shit of a brother would make him suffer for it. Immediately.

Before Terry had the chance to respond, Mandy leapt from the top shelf of a pallet rack and landed on Arnie's back. Her jaws clamped around the back of his neck as if she intended to bite his head clean off.

Terry fell to the floor. He crawled backward away from the scuffle, eyes flashing yellow as fear triggered the beginnings of his own shift. I stepped out from behind the shelf and planted my boot in the middle of his back.

"Sit. Stay," I said, pointing my gun at his face when he glanced over his shoulder. The wilting personality he'd exhibited with Arnie vanished, and his features twisted with loathing.

Arnie's gaze snagged on mine as he fought Mandy, swinging his body wildly to dislodge her. His arms bent at odd angles, hands fisting in her fur. Then he pitched himself forward—at me.

Mandy flipped tail over muzzle, her jaws snapping shut as they lost their hold on Arnie's greasy neck. She slammed into my chest. My gun flew out of my hand, and we both collapsed to the floor, Murphy's damn cape tangling around us.

Terry watched wide-eyed. He'd assumed that the fight was over, but I couldn't tell if he was relieved or disappointed by the notion.

"Go!" Arnie barked, his teeth crowding his mouth as he resisted shifting. He pulled the sawed-off shotgun from under his jacket and took aim while Terry scrambled out of the line of fire.

The pistol I'd dropped was nowhere to be found, but my hand was already on my second. I pulled it as Mandy rolled off me, locking my gaze and aim on Arnie. His snarl stretched wider, but his teeth slowly retracted inside his jaws, accompanied by the grotesque sound of cracking and popping bones.

"I've got this," I said to Mandy. "Get the other one."

She snorted in frustration but hurried after Terry. Firepower had a definite advantage over teeth, and no matter how badly she wanted this fight, she knew the odds were not in her favor.

"Did you miss me, sweetheart?" Arnie leered down at me, his focus as unwavering as mine. The first one to blink would be getting a face full of silver.

"Don't worry," I said, pushing aside the cape with my free hand as I rose to my feet. "I won't miss this time."

"I must say, I'm surprised to see you—out here among the peasants." He leaned to one side, then the other, studying the way the barrel of my gun followed his movement. "Thought your working days were through after you managed to get your foot in House Lilith's gilded door. Or are you just doing most of your *dirty* work behind closed doors now?"

I scoffed. "You're one to talk—"

Something rattled near Arnie's feet, breaking my concentration. It was all the opening he needed.

Our guns went off at the same time. My bullet blasted through a cardboard catering box full of silverware that Arnie had kicked up between us, but his slug hit home—square in the center of my chest.

All the air left my lungs as I fell, and then my head bounced off the concrete floor. Silverware rained down on me. The ballistic vest had stopped the shotgun blast from tearing through my flesh, but the impact still felt like a sucker punch delivered by the Hulk.

My blood vision flickered out. I didn't have the energy or will to sustain it while I fought to stay conscious. My ears rang, and I could do little more than blink like a fish while obliterated bits of cardboard clouded the air above. It looked like falling snow in the thin moonlight that spilled through the window behind Arnie.

He closed the distance in two strides and stomped on my wrist before kicking my gun away. I didn't have enough wind to complain. When I did finally suck in a ragged breath, his nose twitched, and a smirk lit his face.

"I was afraid you might've passed out," he said and then proceeded to strip out of his leather jacket. He tossed it on a work table along with the shotgun. Then he unbuckled his belt.

I tried to sit up, but my head felt loose on my shoulders. The room spun around me, and every breath burned, though they were coming faster now, thanks to my mounting fear.

"Do you know what I do to pretty little bloodsuckers who put their fangs in me without invitation?" Arnie asked in a razor-sharp whisper as he continued undressing.

"You were going to shoot me in that alley behind the Scarlett Inn." I gritted my teeth. My chest throbbed, but the anger kept me grounded. "You and your mangey lot were turning those girls against their will. *You* started this. Don't expect an apology from me."

"I'm not after an apology, sweetheart. But I will have my pound of flesh." His voice took on a gravelly note, and when he turned around, I saw why.

Yellow eyes stared back at me.

Arnie pounced on my chest, deflating my lungs once

again. He was already halfway through his shift. It was much faster than Mandy's.

The crunch of bones assaulted my ears, and his warping features hurt my brain. I pulled my arms up over my face, trying to block out the image, but Arnie's deformed hands clawed at my sleeves, tearing through the thin material as if it were tissue paper.

A second later, there was a massive gray wolf on top of me. I could have sworn it laughed at my terror, just before chomping down on my arm.

A guttural scream tore from my lips as teeth touched bone and set my nerves on fire. My free hand slapped at the rough concrete floor, searching for my gun, but the prongs of a fork bit into my palm instead. The pain hardly registered with wolf fangs shredding my forearm.

I grasped the utensil's handle and stabbed it into the side of Arnie's neck.

His fangs ripping out of my flesh hurt even worse, and I almost blacked out from the bloody dog breath he panted in my face. He shook his muzzle, trying to dislodge the fork, and I took the opportunity to pull my knees up to my chest.

A startled whine rattled through Arnie's fangs as my boots planted on his ribcage, prying him away from me. He snapped at my face and shoulders, but I didn't give him the chance to latch on to me a second time. My legs recoiled, and when he lunged forward, I kicked with everything I had.

Arnie grunted and rose up on his hind legs as he tried to catch himself. At the same time, I rolled onto my side and hiked my leg to deliver a final strike to his chest with the heel of my boot.

The wolf crashed through the window, paws desperately treading air. His yellow eyes were too wide, and they were all I could see within his dark silhouette now that the Eye of Blood had faded. Then he dropped out of sight, leaving behind the moon in the jagged frame of broken glass.

Bloody and broken, I searched the rest of the factory loft, but I couldn't find Mandy.

Murphy was still guarding the stairs leading back to the main floor. The gunfire had dissipated somewhat, but the fight downstairs wasn't over yet, and five bodies lay in a pile on the landing between the two flights. Two of them were naked—wolves who had shifted back to their human forms postmortem.

"Holy shit, Skye." Murphy cringed at my mutilated arm. I couldn't feel my fingers, but I'd reclaimed one of my Reaper TDs and clutched it tightly in my good hand.

"You should see the other guy," I said, unable to muster

a smile. My mouth was dry, and my fangs extended, demanding blood to repair the damage. "Mandy slip by you?"

He nodded and glanced down at the sleeve of his jacket, torn from wrist to elbow. "Chasing after some asshole in a plaid shirt. He snuck up from behind. 'Bout pushed me over the railing."

"He's going to blow the building," I said. "We have to get everyone out."

"What's left of them, you mean."

Murphy stayed close as I headed down the first flight and stepped over Arnie's lifeless henchmen. The sight of the carnage made my stomach churn. I was overwhelmed with disgust and hunger and a horrific vision of myself licking cold blood from the corpses.

I had to get out of here.

The shots downstairs were dying down, like a bag of popcorn finishing its business. There would be fewer distractions to provide cover, but I didn't trust myself to remain on the landing with the dead bodies. And no amount of cover would matter if the building came down on top of us.

I tried to activate the Eye of Blood again. The wash of red flickered in and out like a storm threatening to knock out the power—only the power was me, and the storm was my blood leaking all over the damn place.

"You can't see," I said to Murphy, too frazzled to choose my words with caution. "You should slip out the back door Nicks is guarding and tell him to radio the others to retreat."

"What are you going to do?" Murphy demanded. "You can't see either."

It sounded more like a question, and I watched the confusion blossom on his face in the glow of the security light above the landing. If we survived this, he would want to know how I managed to get us across the room and to the stairs.

"I'm going to find Mandy," I said. "Let's move. We're wasting time." I took off down the stairs, cape flapping behind me.

Murphy didn't look thrilled about my plan, but we didn't have many other options, and there was no way I was leaving my girl behind. He'd have to trust that I could find my way because he couldn't find it for me.

The few agents and wolves who remained on the ground floor were the most cautious of either side. They knew how to take cover and bide their time, picking out a target rather than shooting every which way like Yosemite Sam.

As I descended the bottom flight of stairs, I activated the Eye of Blood long enough to case the pallet racks from overhead. I didn't see Terry or Mandy, but I did spy one of Arnie's men crouched behind a stack of cookware boxes. He glanced up, and I squeezed the trigger.

Murphy's surprised breath wheezed over my shoulder, and he swore as we left the halo of the landing light, the darkness fully embracing us.

Nicks was no longer at the back door, but two of his men still guarded the exit. They took turns firing at the remaining wolves and men, yelling for them to shift or drop their weapons and stand down. The sight of Murphy and me scrambling down the stairs startled them, but they realized who we were before trying to feed us a lead sandwich.

"Go," I said to Murphy, pushing him past the two agents and out of the building. "Find Nicks."

One of the agents at the door reached for me, but a bullet grazed his shoulder. He spun away from me to return fire, and I used the distraction to cut across the room, angling for a faintly lit doorway in the corner.

The exit led out to the loading dock. Two vans were parked inside, but it was the office at the back platform where I found Terry and Mandy, as well as a long table topped with a dozen pressure cookers.

"Get back! I'll do it!" Terry's thumb trembled over the button of what looked to be a garage door opener.

I trained my gun on his head but remained just inside the doorway of the office. Mandy stood a few feet ahead of me, frozen in place. She growled, but I had a feeling it was at me rather than Terry, urging me to get out while I could. She was too far away from the man to stop him if he decided to press the button.

"If you do that, you're just as dead as we are," I said, hoping he wasn't so brainwashed that he had a death wish. That he hesitated was a good sign, but it was no guarantee.

"I have kids," he said as if pleading for his life.

"I imagine they'd like to see their father again. Wouldn't you like to see them, too?"

He shook the detonator, using it to punctuate the words he shouted at me. "I'd *like* to see them live in a world where they don't have to worry about vampires *pushing* them around, *treating* them like second-class citizens."

"That's not what Blood Vice sets out to do." I shook my head, but a part of me wondered if maybe I hadn't seen enough of the underworld to know what I was talking about. I couldn't confess that to Trigger Happy Terry, though.

"My brother was an agent." His voice broke, and he paused to swallow. "Got nicked by a killer vamp first week on the job."

"What a coincidence," I said. "Same thing happened to me."

"Know where that killer vamp is now?" he asked, not waiting for me to take a guess. "They returned him to his sire. Treated him like a fucking puppy that had gotten loose and nipped the mailman's ankle. My brother's wife got an apology, a check, and a devasted kid she had to raise by herself."

"Officers die in the line of duty all the time," I said, inching closer to Mandy. "I did. My mother did. We knew the risks. What more could Blood Vice have offered your sister-in-law to make this right?"

"I don't know." Terry scoffed. "How about *justice*?"

"Is that what you think you'll get by blowing up a bunch of innocent people?"

"Innocent?" Spit webbed between his lips, and his eyes flickered yellow. "The duke is the one who signed the fucking check!" His teeth gnashed, and his jaw bowed out unnaturally. It was unsettling, and I wasn't sure what I could say without making it worse.

"What can I do?" I asked. I was prepared to lie through my teeth and offer him anything he wanted to get the detonator out of his hand. Mandy was too close. Hell, anyone still in the building was too close. "Make a demand. You wanna get out of here? We could get you an armored truck."

Terry laughed through clenched teeth. The sound dropped my heart into my stomach.

"House Lilith owes my family a blood debt, and it's time to pay."

I dropped my gun and threw myself over Mandy as he pressed the button.

Chapter Twenty

The blood in my mouth was familiar, like comfort food. It reminded me of the chicken noodle soup my mother used to serve me in bed when I was a kid—minus the chicken and the noodles. But hey, it was the thought that counted, right? The intent. That's what I tasted in Mandy's blood.

And also hair.

I came to, gagging and sputtering, and found Mandy's furry body curled in next to mine under Murphy's cape. The garment had shielded us from the worst of the explosion, but falling debris was another story.

My head throbbed, and blood dripped over one of my eyebrows. The arm Arnie had used as a chew toy curled uselessly against my chest. Mandy chewed at one of her front paws, digging out a piece of mangled metal. From the amount of blood that coated my throat, I was sure she'd let the wound bleed a while before tending to it.

Wooden beams and chunks of concrete pressed in all around us—and also a fair amount of light slipping through gaps in the broken building. The illumination moved, and I heard a familiar voice shout my name.

"Your Highness! Please, you should stay clear of the structure. There could be more bombs," Nicks shouted.

"If you put your hands on me, I'll tear them off and slap

some sense into you with them," Ursula yelled back. "Jenna! Mandy? Are you in there?"

"Jenna!" Dante joined in, and I heard Nicks groan in desperation.

"We're working as fast as we can to clear the scene, Your Grace."

"And you're doing a great job, but you must work faster," Dante said in true duke fashion, even if his voice were laced with thinly veiled panic. "Jenna!" he called again.

"Dante," I said, my words weak and wet with Mandy's blood. I swallowed and tried again. "We're over here."

A board creaked above my head, and I used my good arm to pull the cape up over Mandy and me as more debris rained down on us. Then a spotlight shined in my face.

"Jenna!" Ursula reached inside the pocket we were trapped in and seized my arm, pulling me out as if I weighed no more than a handful of wet laundry. She wrapped her arms around me and squeezed until I cried out in pain. Everything hurt, and I could hardly stand on my own two feet.

Dante was gentler, slipping his arm behind my back to steady me. He ran his thumb over my bloody eyebrow and let his fingertips trail behind my ear and down the side of my neck.

"What am I going to do with you?" he said, his breath hitching with shaky relief.

I didn't have an answer. My head was still reeling, trying to reassemble the pieces of the night. Agents with flashlights circled the ruins of the factory, searching for survivors. Several more Blood Vice SUVs lined the surrounding streets, and police tape marked off the block.

"Mandy." I reached behind me for her, but she leapt through the gap on her own, whimpering when she landed on her injured paw.

"Get a stretcher," Nicks hollered at a pair of agents. Mandy growled under her breath at him. She'd sooner shit in his front lawn—in human form—than get carried off a job as a victim.

"Here," I said, slipping off Murphy's cape and folding it over her back as she limped past me. She'd want something warm to cover up with after shifting.

"Skye!" Murphy climbed over a downed sheet of metal roofing. "I'm so sorry. I should have stayed with you."

"Did you get to Nicks in time?" I asked.

"I did, but—"

"But nothing. You did exactly what you should've."

Dante squeezed Murphy's shoulder. I wasn't sure if he agreed with me, but considering that we were all intact—more or less—he was willing to let tonight be a success. Murphy still looked ashamed, but he heaved a sigh and nodded. His eyes searched mine for answers that I wasn't ready to give him yet, but I decided that I would. Soon.

Ursula poked a finger at my wounded arm. "You need blood," she said as if the thought hadn't crossed my mind.

"Yup," I said tightly, pulling my angry limb away from her talons.

Mandy had bled enough to reanimate me for the time being, but my fangs ached for a *real* drink. Or three. I would need that much if I wanted use of my ruined hand anytime soon.

Nicks led us away from the wreckage and toward his SUV. Dozens more vehicles came and went, and I imagined the new agents on the scene were mostly wolves and half-sireds there to replace the vampires heading off to wherever they died for the day. I was ready to do the same.

Lady Beauclair crossed the street to join us as we reached Nicks' ride. She'd added a white fur coat over her pantsuit. The flashing police lights in the SUV's dash splashed it with red and blue.

"Your Grace." She gasped and pressed a hand to her chest as she took in my face and arm.

"Present." I tried to smile, but everything hurt too much.

"Speaking of presents—" Nicks rapped his knuckles on the passenger door and then pointed at the back seat. The window rolled down slowly, revealing Arnie's battered face and naked chest. He was covered in cuts and shivering with rage. The cuffs around his wrist were secured to a bar across the back of the front seat, and they rattled as he tried to lunge through the window at us.

"You think you've won?" He howled with manic laughter. "The Moreau Pack is a thousand strong. You can't stop us all, and we won't stop. Not until the blood runs free."

"We'll take this one to Denver to stand trial," Lady Beauclair said.

"Fuck you and your circus." Arnie spat on her coat. "My brother will free me, and then we'll free the blood. Free the blood! Free the blood! Free the blood!"

Nicks knocked on the passenger door again, and Arnie's hateful chanting was snuffed out as the window slid back into place.

"We've put out warrants for Marcel Moreau and all of his known associates that weren't accounted for tonight," Nicks said, glancing over his shoulder where agents were busy loading bodies into the back of an SUV. My eyes settled on a blood-caked limb, and my stomach knotted.

God, I needed some serious therapy.

"I trust this means the evaluation is complete and satisfactory?" Ursula said as Lady Beauclair dabbed at the wet spot on her coat.

"Well, I'll have to consult with the others," she began, seeming taken aback by the princess's timing. "There are many factors to consider—"

"You said if I solved this case, you'd leave us in peace." I glared at the plastic smile the councilwoman offered.

"I *said* I would as long as nothing damning was discovered during the harem and guard interviews."

"What's your problem?" I snapped. "Did someone make your scionic youth a living hell, and now you feel it's your duty to continue the cycle?"

"*Your Grace*," she said in a scolding tone. "Surely, your sire has educated you on the consequences of making false accusations against members of noble households."

Noble. Such a relative term in undead society.

Threatening a blood duel, even subtly, was a low blow. I was sure Beauclair knew about Vanessa Sorano's retracted challenge, as well.

"My education and sire are first class." I ground my teeth and mirrored her fake smile. "But that was a question, my lady. Not an accusation. I just survived a gunfight and an explosion. If you're trying to get a rise out of me, you'll have to do better than that."

"Dawn is approaching, my dear," Dante said, ending the conversation by opening a hand toward the car waiting at the curb. "Mr. Murphy, would you instruct Lane to drive the council lady back to the manor?"

Murphy nodded. "Will do, boss."

"And offer him my most sincere apologies," Dante added, ignoring the hateful look Beauclair shot him.

His insults were so much smoother than mine. Maybe I'd convince him to teach me some of those moves along with the history lessons he planned to take over.

I managed to put down two pots of fresh blood before dying in Dante's embrace. Ursula hadn't tried to stop him when he carried me off to his room after Murphy had taken us home. In fact, she'd offered to check in on Audrey before turning in for the day herself.

Mandy looked much better after her shift. Her arm was still bruised where a chunk of shrapnel from the explosion had struck her, but one of Nicks' guys had wrapped it for her. If it were fractured, she'd need to shift another time or two before it would heal fully.

Dante had insisted that she ride with us. He'd sent a couple of the wolf guards—the pair that Mandy had referred to as Tweedledee and Tweedledum when we first shacked up with the duke—to collect the car she'd commandeered to join the raid.

Sunday evening, I rose feeling less *Nosferatu* but not quite *Twilight*. But I could at least wiggle my fingers again, and

Dante brought me blood in bed. He even adorned the cute little lap tray with a vase of fresh daisies and the updated case file for the opera house investigation.

"I *thought* Tracy Young's vehicle seemed familiar," I said, setting my cup of blood down on the tray so I could grasp the open folder with both hands. "Polly Hughes cited it in her amended report."

The Blood Vice lab had given Young's SUV the white-glove treatment and found hair and blood evidence in the back seat that matched the murdered girls from Bathory House. Making Bart Haulette Phillip Salinger's accomplice.

"Yes. Miss Watts and Miss Kelley can finally rest in peace now," Dante said. He planted a kiss on my temple and topped off my cup. Then he circled the bed to stand in front of his mirrored armoire where he finished buttoning his dress shirt.

It wasn't much of a surprise that the Moreau Pack had had a hand in the killings. We already knew about their working relationship with Kassandra—they'd attacked us on her behalf after Ursula's trial last year. What bothered me was that they were still a pain in House Lilith's ass *after* Kassandra had been stuffed into a coffin.

So now, the question I found myself asking was: *Who's driving this thing?* Was Marcel playing henchman to Kassandra or vice versa? How many pieces did this damn puzzle have? And whose bright idea was it to take it out of the box in the first place?

Last, but not least, I wanted to know which pencil-pusher at Blood Vice had botched my name on the report.

"Jenni Skype?" I turned the folder around to show Dante. "Can I fire this clown?"

"I believe Captain Nicks already tried that once." His reflection smirked at me in the mirror.

I made a face at him and dropped the file back on the tray before picking up my cup of blood. The elixir was honey in my mouth—much tastier than the cold, tacky cadaver blood I'd been hankering for that morning, I was sure.

Life was beginning to feel normal again. Pleasant, even. Now, if the council could just make like a guillotine and head off, I'd give this night a perfect score.

When I finally decided to get dressed and venture out of Dante's bedroom, I found Lady Peyroux admiring my portrait of Ursula in the foyer. I almost tried to slip past her on my way to check on Laura, but she noticed me right away as if she'd been waiting.

"Congratulations on solving the case," she said by way of greeting. "We are all quite impressed—even Regina, despite her abrasiveness."

"Does this mean we've passed the evaluation?" I asked, forgoing the regal small talk and getting right to it. I was so tired of the fancy gobbledygook that came with being a royal scion. It was pretentious and annoying.

"You're in the clear," Peyroux confirmed. "And I would very much like to hire you to do a portrait for me. The duke mentioned you have experience as a sketch artist."

"Not really—I mean, I never did it professionally."

"You are a natural talent," she said. "It is a shame that you wish to nurture your more violent gifts."

I gave her a tight smile. "My violent gifts save lives— possibly even yours."

"For which I am grateful," Peyroux said, placing a hand over her heart to express her sincerity. "Truthfully. I only meant that I fear the loss of this talent"—she turned back to the portrait of Ursula—"should your other fail you. I would love to see my sire brought to life on the canvas again."

"Sure. I can do that."

"Ladies," DeAngelo greeted us as he entered the foyer. One of the council guards carried his luggage. "Our time draws to a close, I'm afraid."

"So soon?" I asked, imitating his faux cheer and enjoying the way it ruffled his feathers. "Are you sure the Nightfall Opera House case is well and closed? Should we assemble the troops and launch a crusade to seek out Marcel Moreau and these dastardly Free Blooders tonight?"

DeAngelo snorted. "Without his beta henchman, Marcel is vulnerable. His illegal operations will suffer, and he will have to show his face to rally fresh support. I have faith that Blood Vice will capture him eventually—perhaps even you will be instrumental in locating him, as you were with your sire."

I wasn't sure if he was complimenting me or making a jab. I'd hunted down Ursula to secure my freedom and ended up under her thumb instead. No good deed went unpunished, I guessed. Although, the sentence was bothering me less and less, even with the princess's mood swings.

Dante appeared in the doorway of his office. "Your car awaits," he told Peyroux and DeAngelo. Both councilors bowed first to Dante and then to me before heading for the entrance.

A guard opened the front door for them. Outside in the driveway, Beauclair climbed into a limo as the driver put her luggage in the trunk. More luggage—Peyroux's, I assumed—waited on the porch. The guard toting DeAngelo's leather suitcase took up one of the paisley duffle bags in his free hand to speed the departure along.

I leaned against the open doorway, arms folded, breathing in the winter air. It smelled sweeter tonight, tinged with victory and freedom. Dante slipped in beside me, and together we watched as the limo pulled out of the driveway.

"Lady Butt Hair was certainly in a hurry to leave," I said, caressing Dante's hand where it rested on my hip. "She didn't even say goodbye."

The duke sniffed, and his lips quirked with a sly grin. "I informed her of Ursula's successful outing at Bleeders. The princess is reestablishing her reputation among vampiric society, and as such, the council will be met with resistance if they continue this unwarranted witch hunt against a member of the royal family who has already suffered more than her fair share."

"And that irked her enough that she decided to wait outside for her car?"

"No," Dante confessed. "She chose that course of action after I told her that any additional political assault against the royal family would be grounds for a motion to revoke House Beauclair's seat on the council for abuse of power."

"Salty. I like it." I grinned and draped my arms over his shoulders.

Dante leaned in for a kiss, but before our mouths met, headlights splashed across us and the front of the manor as a car pulled into the drive. I retreated to my side of the open doorway for fear our council guests had returned for some forgotten item or insult. But as the vehicle curled sideways and parked before the front steps, I realized it was not the same limo.

The car's back door opened, and a face I hadn't expected to ever see again squinted up at me.

"Your hair…it's…it's…" David Steckleman stammered as he crept up the porch steps. His gaze slid to Dante, and he froze. "You're not really thinking of leaving me for this pool boy, are you?"

"Pool boy?" Dante bristled, and his hand reclaimed my waist. "Do you know this man, Jenna?"

"Jenna?" David's voice rose an octave. "But…you're dead. I was at your funeral."

"Shit." I gritted my teeth as the two guards in the foyer stepped in behind Dante and me, their hands not-so-subtly slipping inside their jackets. "Wait! He's my sister's ex-boyfriend."

"Fiancé," David countered.

"Right, my sister's ex-fiancé."

"It was a little spat," he protested. "Hardly worth calling off the wedding."

"You threatened to kill her with bad sushi!" I pointed a finger in his face, my civility crumbling the same way it had the first two times I'd met the pompous prick.

"I wasn't *serious*," David said. His eyes bulged at the same moment I felt my fangs dig into my bottom lip, but before things got too weird, my sister pushed through the guards and past Dante and me.

"David? You're really here." Laura cleared her throat and propped her hands on her hips, trying to appear casual despite her labored breathing. "I mean, *what* are you doing here?"

"How did he *find* here?" I added through clenched teeth and shot Laura a wide-eyed glare.

"You posted a picture online with that foster girl who was staying with your late—*uh*—apparently still living sister," David said. "I looked up her address on the guest list— though I must say, I didn't expect to find her in *this* neighborhood."

"That's because you're a prejudiced asshat," I offered, ignoring the dirty look Laura gave me.

"I came for you," David said, taking Laura's hand as he knelt on the stairs at her feet. He reached into his pocket and produced an obnoxiously oversized diamond ring. "I'll always come for you."

Laura's lashes brimmed with tears as he slid the ring onto her finger. "Oh, that's the sweetest—" She covered her mouth with one hand and swallowed a few times before finally pulling away from him to vomit in the bushes that bordered the front porch. Her retching was so loud that we all took a step back.

David's soap-opera smolder wilted at the sight, but he offered her his silk pocket square once she'd finished regurgitating her latest meal. "I guess this means the pregnancy wasn't a stunt, after all."

"No, it wasn't." Laura sobbed and rubbed her face clean with the handkerchief. "I'm going to be fat and miserable by this summer. We have to call the wedding off. I can't be seen in a white dress like that. Think of the tabloid pictures!"

"We'll reschedule," David said. "Move the date up."

"It's no use. Look"—Laura waved a hand at her perfectly flat stomach—"I'm already showing. Everyone will know!"

"We can go to the courthouse first thing in the morning." He took Laura's hand again and petted it as if it were a kitten. "Or we can fly to Vegas or Jamaica—wherever you want to go."

I threw my arms up into the air. "Oh, sure. Whisk her off again. That's just great."

Dante cleared his throat, drawing everyone's attention back to the doorway. "I might have a better idea," he said with a devious grin.

Chapter Twenty-one

There was something very wrong, but also very right, about standing beside my sister as she vowed to have and to hold David Steckleman—for richer or poorer, at that.

Glowing patio heaters dotted the backyard and sat on top of the tables the guards had carried outside for the harem to arrange and decorate with vases of heather and pale roses. The white string lights still adorning the house lent extra ambiance, too. I was suddenly glad that Audrey had begged to keep them up as long as possible.

The future baroness also had Levi set up her keyboard near the back door so she could play the wedding march for Laura before Lane took over DJ duty. And Belinda had hired a new caterer—now that Hearty Harem was in the ground and off the menu—to put together a light dinner and an elegant cake dotted with elaborate frosting flowers.

I was blown away by how much work everyone had put into making this happen—and on such short notice. Laura was, too. Her eyes watered as she took everything in, walking down the makeshift aisle in one of Ursula's white evening gowns and a red guard cape.

Bomb-resistant *and* fashionable. Truly the best of both worlds.

My sister was a surprisingly believable blushing bride,

though I hadn't made up my mind if that was due to her acting chops or if she actually loved Hollywood for more than the fame and financial stability he represented. Sure, I could admit that he wasn't half bad-looking. For a senior citizen. But that wasn't really something I could give Laura grief over now that I was pretend hitched to a vampire a century and a half old.

Dante stood in as Hollywood's best man, grinning at me like a Cheshire cat from his side of the improvised altar while one of the harem donors officiated the ceremony.

We'd convinced my sister's fiancé that we were secret agents who'd had to fake our deaths to go undercover. It wasn't the most original cover story, but it was close enough to the truth that I wouldn't have felt bad about the lie even if I liked Hollywood. Luckily, he was too smitten with my sister to bother asking all the other obvious questions.

Couldn't the ceremony wait until the sun came up? Why are half the guests skipping dinner and drinking red wine instead of champagne? Do these people look a little anemic to you?

We would have come up with something—hell, we'd just bullshitted our way through the council's evaluation. Though really, in the end, it hadn't been bullshit at all.

Ursula wasn't an ideal sire, and I wasn't a perfect scion. So what? Did such things even exist? We were making the arrangement work, and yeah, there was a learning curve. But we'd survived the first year without killing each other. I gave myself permission to be proud of that fact.

And the fact that I was about to wing a maid of honor toast like a boss.

"To Laura, my beautiful, glowing sister," I said, holding up my champagne flute of blood. "I can't tell you how happy I am to be sharing this moment with you. It's even better than the Barbie destination beach wedding of '97, though the guests had pretty spectacular hair that summer."

Laura's face turned red, and she pressed her lips together. She'd wanted to be a lot of things as a little girl, but none of her hopeful occupations had been as problematic as her desire to be a hairdresser—and she'd had an uncanny knack for locating scissors. She'd butchered all of our dolls, her own hair, and mine before that year was over.

And to Holl—*David*," I corrected myself. "My…charming brother-in-law. We don't know each other well, and since I'm legally dead and you live a couple thousand miles away, we probably *won't* get to know each other much better. But know this. As long as you take good care of my sister, you're all right in my book."

I left off the *what-if* scenario detailing the way his body would be found if he *didn't* take good care of Laura. I was sure he could fill in the blank.

Mandy took a turn offering a toast—including a few well-wishes and polite demands on behalf of Duncan, who spent the night in the crook of her arm. By the end of the night, Sweet Pea had claimed her place on Mandy's opposite arm. I had to laugh. Her alpha wolf front could only hold up for so long where pint-sized pups were concerned.

After dinner, the dancing began. Dante twirled me around for a few songs, and then we made our getaway through the sliding door to his bedroom. A small fire crackled in the fireplace, providing just enough light for us to find our way to the bed. With the council long gone, we couldn't wait one more second.

Dante's lips brushed my throat. His breath warmed my skin and sent a chill through me at the same time. I threaded my fingers through his hair, breaking up the stiff curls he'd slicked back for the ceremony. I wanted him unruly and wild, as natural as he appeared whenever we woke from our unnatural slumber.

"Do you love me, Jenna?" he whispered against my neck.

"Of course I do."

"Am I enough?" The question was so vulnerable, it caused my breath to hitch. "Without the light of day, without wedding cake or children. Am I enough?" he asked again.

"You're more than enough. So much more," I sighed as Dante's lips returned to my skin and moved down my neck to my chest.

"You are everything I have been waiting for, and I have been so very patient," he said, pulling at the silk ribbon that laced up the back of my dress. I unknotted his tie and used the loose ends to pull his face up to mine, smothering his sweet nothings with a kiss.

I never wanted to take this for granted. Not in a hundred years. Not in a thousand.

Dante's hands pushed my dress up my thighs, but when he settled between my legs, he went rigid. His breath rasped at the back of his throat as though he were choking, and his eyes blinked up at the ceiling, pain creasing his brow.

"Dante? Dante!" I sat upright and grabbed the front of his open dress shirt as he began to fall away from me. "What's happening?"

"I do not...I do not know."

My mind raced with every awful question it could summon. Could vampires have seizures? Had someone spiked our blood? Was he dying? Was there really nothing I could do to make this nightmare stop?

"Dante... I don't know what to do," I cried and pulled him in close to me as he trembled. When his arms wrapped around my back, a sob of relief shuddered past my lips.

"Jenna," he breathed my name. There was still pain in his voice, but he had control of his body again. I clutched him tighter, unable to let go after such a scare. "Jenna," he panted again. "I can see…*everything*."

Music trickled in from outside as the patio door opened, and Ursula entered Dante's room. She held a champagne flute of blood in one hand and Laura's toss-away bouquet in her other. The relaxed joy in her expression vanished as her gaze fell on Dante's stricken expression.

"No," she whispered, realizing his suffering before he put it into words.

"The prince has departed. My world is dressed in his blood."

See how it all ends in…

OUT FOR BLOOD

BLOOD VICE BOOK EIGHT

Coming 2020

Jenna thought thwarting the Free Blooders' terrorist plans in St. Louis would send the bloodthirsty rebels back into the shadows. But the organization's reach was much farther than anyone realized. When more bomb attacks sweep the country, taking out high-profile vampires at every turn, House Lilith and the Vampiric High Council must act fast if they're to maintain control over supernatural society. If the Free Blooders succeed, they intend to declare war on humanity. And they won't stop until the blood runs free.

ACKNOWLEDGMENTS

Thank you to all the amazing peeps who helped make this book shine: Chelle Olson, my wonderful, patient, sharp-eyed editor; Rebecca Frank, my magic-weaving cover designer; my critique group, the Four Horsemen of the Bookocalypse, whom I adore for their friendship, feedback, epic books, and good looks; my Grim Readers, who offered encouragement and pain relief advice as I struggled to write this one through an especially achy winter; THE professor, George Shelley, for the proofreading, thoughtful feedback, and coffee book talks that I always look forward to; my Xavi baby, who made sure I got plenty of snuggles and kisses during breaks; and my husband Paul, Pollywog, Daddy Feller, my better half, who lets me tell him all my secrets and plans and doesn't shout "Spoiler Alert!" in my face (too often). I love that you enjoy my work and want to be surprised when you're proofreading it. And I adore you for how often you give up that surprise to be my sounding board. You are so much more than I ever hoped to find in a life partner. I love you.

Extra special thanks this round to my BFF and virtual assistant, Karen Gomez, who took a lot of work off my plate while I finished this book. You are amazing! I'm so excited to be working with you!

And finally, I owe a grateful shout out to Big Brother for not storming my castle after all the bomb research I did for this book. I swear, I don't even own a pressure cooker—no matter how many times the spybot ads try to sell me one now.

ABOUT THE AUTHOR

USA Today bestselling fantasy author **Angela Roquet** is a great big weirdo. She lives in Missouri with her husband and son in a house stuffed with books, toys, skulls, owls, and glitter-speckled craft supplies. She's a member of SFWA and HWA, as well as the Four Horsemen of the Bookocalypse, her epic book critique group, where she's known as Death. When not swearing at the keyboard, she enjoys boating with her family at Lake of the Ozarks and reading books that raise eyebrows. You can find Angela online at **www.angelaroquet.com**

If you enjoyed this book, please leave a review. Your support and feedback are greatly appreciated!

www.ingramcontent.com/pod-product-compliance
Lightning Source LLC
Chambersburg PA
CBHW050346190726
48284CB00007BB/2168